I0719524

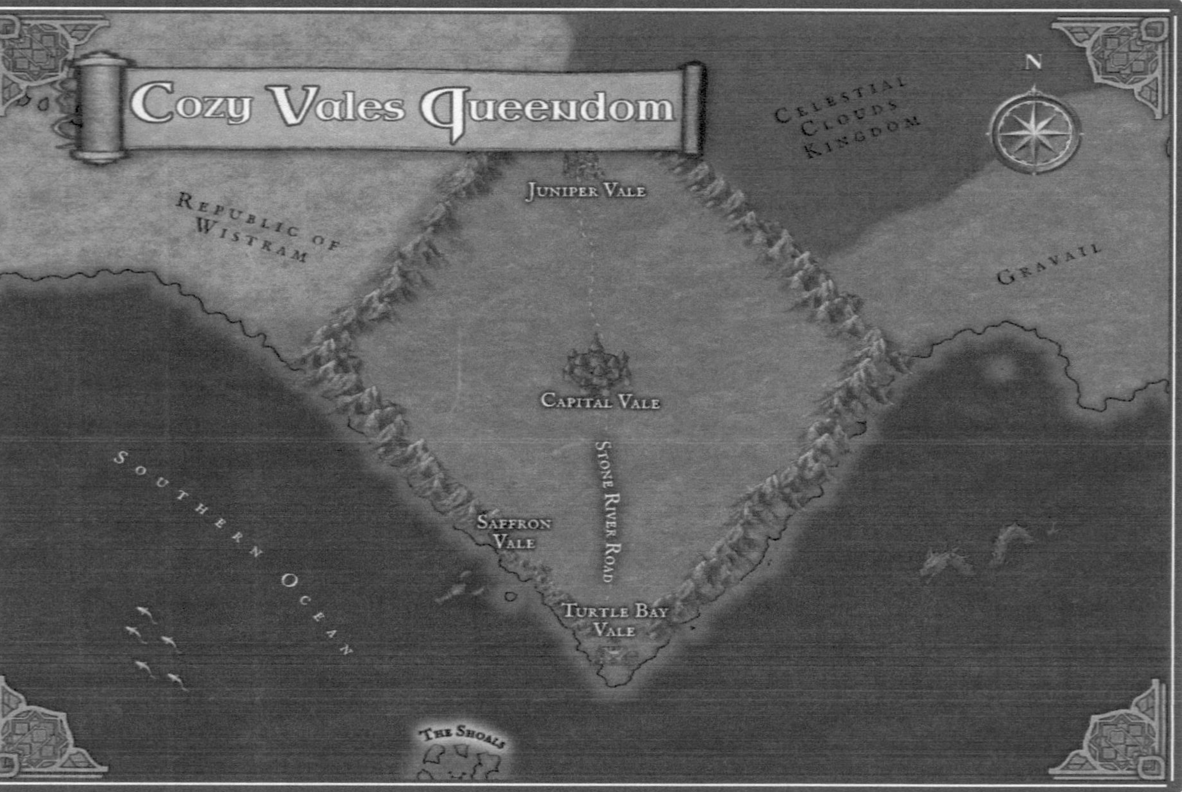

Cozy Vales Queendom
N
Celestial Clouds Kingdom
Republic of Wistram
Juniper Vale
Gravail
Capital Vale
Stone River Road
Southern Ocean
Saffron Vale
Turtle Bay Vale
The Shoals

Saffron Vale
N
Rainbow River
Cheese Rolling Hill
Dyeing Pools
Crocus Fields
Woolton
Hot Springs
Great Lobster Cove
Southern Ocean
Wyrm Rock

Saffron Vale Series – Book 3

Commission Impossible

A Cozy Vales Story

G Clatworthy

1 2 3 4 5 6 7 8 9 10

ISBN: 978-1-915516-44-2

Published by G Clatworthy

www.gemmaclatworthy.com

gemma@gemmaclatworthy.com

Manufactured by IngramSpark

Australia: Ingram Content Group AU Pty Ltd, Melbourne, Victoria.

US: Lightning Source LLC, La Vergne, Tennessee / Allentown, Pennsylvania / Jackson, Tennessee, United States.

UK: Lightning Source UK Ltd, Milton Keynes, United Kingdom.
Europe: Lightning Source UK Ltd, with facilities in Germany, France, and Spain.

The authorized representative in the European Economic Area for EU GPSR is Lightning Source France

1 Av. Johannes Gutenberg, 78310 Maurepas, France
compliance@lightningsource.fr

This book was manufactured using paper and ink products in accordance with commercial standards.

Foreword

A massive thank you to the Cozy Vales scribes who read this and provided all the support and encouragement in creating Crimson's story. This wouldn't exist without you.

A special thank you to my amazing typo hunters, grammar gurus, and plot pickers who got this story to where it is today. You are awesome!

If you want to support Gemma, you can find her on www.patreon.com/G_Clatworthy for exclusive first reads of new stories. You can also join her newsletter at www.gemmaclatworthy.com for a free prequel to the Saffron Vale series and follow Gemma on www.instagram.com/gemmaclatworthy,

www.facebook.com/gemmaclatworthy or join the reader's group on Facebook: Gemma's book wyrms.

An extract from Intara's Guide to Cozy Vales –
Highlights and Summaries of my Time in the
Queendom

Saffron Vale is named for the crocus flowers that grow there. It is known throughout the queendom for its brightly coloured cloth and excellent dyes. It is unsurprising, then, that its local cuisine includes spices that add colour as well as flavour and I implore you to try the yellow saffron cake – a yeasty cake stuffed with currants and other dried fruits that is a buttercup yellow colour.

I first tasted this delicacy in the Cozy Lobster café in Woolton – the main town in the vale – where I also sampled a half-moon shaped savoury pastry called a 'pasty' (pronounced colloquially as 'paasty', which was both filling and delicious.

You may well choose to pair it with scrumpy – an alcoholic apple drink that is well known in this vale. Each orchard here has its own recipe, and the drink varies in taste from sharp to so sweet you would hardly guess it contained alcohol.

When I inquired about the name of the café, I was told it was named after a great lobster who has visited this vale since time immemorial, but though I wandered through both Lower and Upper Gull's Bottom – once a small village, now part of the outskirts of the town – to the beach, I didn't catch a glimpse of this famous visitor.

Another export is the rainbow trout, a fish native to the river that flows from the mountains in this vale right to the sea. It is said that the scales are so colourful as a result of the hues that leak into the river as part of the dyeing process. This seems to do no damage to the fish or local wildlife except to imbue them with colour. One of the best sights in this vale is the elusive rainbow river that occurs when conditions are just right and the dyes, instead of combining in swirls, flow instead in almost straight lines down the river. I was fortunate enough to witness this event during my visit and can confirm that it is indeed glorious.

Intara's Guide to Cozy Vales – Highlights and Summaries
of my time in the Queendom

Chapter 1

~ An announcement~

CRIMSON SPAT OUT HER tea and coughed. Several heads turned in the Cozy Lobster café, the busiest – and only – café in Woolton, and looked at her with concern.

"Could you repeat that?" she gasped when she thought she could talk again.

Her friend, Ayla, tucked her long hair behind one of her pointed ears and repeated her announcement. "I'm getting married!" Her grin spread across her elvish face, and she held up a large diamond necklace for Crimson to see. "It's an engagement present!"

Crimson leaned forward and studied the cut diamond necklace that flashed like fire in the light streaming through the café's windows. "When you said you had some big news, I wasn't expecting that."

Ayla took the diamond back and held it up, making a rainbow spark across the table. "Isn't he the best? What did you think I wanted to tell you?"

"That you were going to open a bakery here."

"I'm doing that too. I spoke to Dad, and we've been thinking about expanding out from Juniper Vale for a while, but Capital City has so many bakeries already."

Dilly, the petalborn owner of the café, plonked two plates of cakes on the table. "We've already got a bakery in Woolton."

Crimson winced. Dilly's brother, Duncan, owned the Cozy Lobster bakery next door.

Ayla simply dropped her pendant back around her neck and smiled. "It won't be right away. I'm planning to enjoy our engagement and then we might travel for the honeymoon. Maybe I can work with the current owner. How are his cakes?"

Dilly scoffed and folded her arms. "I'm telling you right now, unless you can make a decent pasty, your bakery doesn't stand a chance here. We don't go for pretentious elvish cakes. People here like honest bakes that fill their stomachs when a squall blows through." Her Saffron Vale accent became more pronounced as her voice rose in defence of her brother's bakery.

"It's alright, Dilly. Ayla wouldn't step on anyone's toes.

Besides, she'll be busy arranging her wedding to…" Crimson trailed off. She hadn't actually asked Ayla who the lucky man was. Maybe her friend had found someone else…she could only hope.

"Jojo" Ayla sighed and clasped her hands together with a dreamy, unfocused look on her face. "Or Maire Bowan as you all call him here." She giggled.

So, she hadn't found someone else. And Crimson would never call the maire Jojo. But didn't satyrs have magic? Maybe he'd enchanted her. Because there was no way her gorgeous friend could decide to live out her life with a dumpy satyr prone to verbal diarrhoea. Surely not. And they hadn't known each other that long. This was fast. Magically fast. Could satyrs make people fall in love with them? No. Crimson shook her head to dispel the foolish thought.

She had researched satyr magic when her friend started dating the maire, and they could only inspire wild joy in others, not enchant people to love them. Ayla must love the maire for himself. Strange as that may be in Crimson's eyes.

Dilly's eyes widened. "Well, congratulations, I guess. I'm sure you'll have a happy life together." The petalborn bustled off to serve someone else, her purple hair bobbing behind her.

Ayla beamed at Crimson. "Do you want to know the best part?"

"There's a best part?"

"Silly." The elf swatted Crimson on the arm before taking a

sip of her tea. "I'll need a wedding dress."

Crimson nodded along.

"And I want you to make it."

Crimson's cup clattered in her hands, and she put it on the table. "Ayla–"

"Don't even think about saying no. Money's no object. Both Jojo and I agree that there are more important things than money." She sighed. "He's so wise." Her gaze snapped back into focus. "Please say yes. I know you don't like him, but–"

"I like him," Crimson protested.

"You haven't even said congratulations."

"Sorry. I guess him trying to shut my shop down last year has stuck with me." She took a deep breath. "Congratulations." Crimson stood and wrapped her arms around her friend, pulling her into a tight hug. Now the word was out, it was easier to feel happy for her friend. The maire might not be her first choice of life partner, but she wasn't the one marrying him, and Ayla knew what she wanted.

"Don't worry so much. This is a good thing. And it means I'm staying in Saffron Vale with him. We get to spend time together again."

"How did you get to be so wise?"

Ayla shrugged. "It must be an elf thing. We live for so long, we get wise."

"But you're not that much older than me, are you?"

Ayla smiled, took a sip of her tea, and avoided the question, as always. "Old enough to know that Jojo's the one for me."

Crimson gave a tight smile. Opposites attracted, so it seemed.

"Now, when are we going to set you up with someone?"

Crimson sipped her tea, her grip tightening on the handle of the mug and inhaled the calming chamomile aroma. She'd thought she'd found someone. They'd shared a passionate kiss that had curled her toes and made her stomach flutter. And then he'd breakfasted with another woman. Crimson sighed.

Maybe there was something about her that meant men betrayed her. First, her best friend had ruined her first shot at getting into the Dressmakers' Guild[1], and now, the man she might have…liked…had gone with someone else. And he'd had the audacity to ask her what was wrong when she'd shut herself in the carriage for the final day's journey home from Capital City.

A warm tongue on her leg jolted Crimson from her introspection, and she reached down to stroke Smudge's head. The small dragon wriggled under her hand in pleasure before he bounded across the room. Crimson paled as she saw who he'd run up to.

---

[1] Fear not, dear reader, Crimson did indeed make it into the guild on her second attempt, where she won a sewing competition. You can read about it in Going for Guild.

Chapter 2

~ *Ayla knows her heart* ~

IEF. AS IF HER thoughts about their kiss had summoned him, there he was, standing in the doorway as if nothing had happened.

"Smudge! Come back."

The dragon ignored her. *Traitor.*

Lief wandered over with a sheepish smile on his stupid, handsome face. Stubble had no right to look that attractive. Scruffy. That was it. He looked like he'd just got out of bed. Crimson felt her cheeks heat, remembering the last time they'd been in bed together. She forced her face into a frown.

"Morning ladies." He handed Smudge to Crimson. "I believe this belongs to you."

"Morning." She couldn't ignore him when he was right next

to her and shoving a dragon onto her lap. But she could keep her sentences to one word.

"That looks like Dilly's celebration cake. What's the big news?"

"I'm getting married," Ayla squealed, holding her pendant up again.

"Congratulations. Maire Bowan is a lucky man."

Ayla blushed happily. "He is. And I'm lucky too. You're invited to the wedding, of course. Everyone is. We just need a date." She shot a sly glance at Crimson. "And Crimson's designing my dress."

Crimson pulled her mouth into something that might pass for a smile and drank some more tea.

"She's very talented," Lief said, his dark eyes sparkling.

"Yes, she is."

Ayla's faith in her should have been comforting, but instead it made Crimson squirm in her seat. She didn't want Lief's attention on her. So, she sipped her tea, knowing that there wasn't enough chamomile in the queendom to quell her churning stomach.

After a long pause, which Crimson refused to fill, Lief's expression flattened, and he gave a stiff bow. "Have a good day, ladies."

"Thank goodness he's gone," Crimson said. Ayla regarded her with curiosity. Crimson hurried on before her friend had a chance to say anything or try to meddle. "So, what are you thinking for your dress? Silk? Satin? Lace?"

As she named materials, design ideas trailed through her head in visions of white and green, or maybe yellow or purple. So much choice.

Ayla's face got that dreamy look again. "Something amazing. Everything you make is so beautiful."

Crimson laid a hand over her friend's, pulling Ayla back to the present. "You're sure?"

The elf gave her a knowing smile. "I'm a one-satyr elf and I'm only getting married once." She patted Crimson's hand. "Yes. I'm sure. Don't worry about me, I know my heart."

Ayla said the last words with an emphasis that made Crimson frown. Crimson knew her own heart, too, and she did not want it broken, not when she still had the scars from Namu's betrayal searing through her. So, instead of opening up to her friend, she changed the subject. "And what have you got planned so far?"

"Jojo wants to make sure it's a celebration to remember. I'm sure you'll come up with something. Anyway, I'd better dash. Jojo wants to show me his latest design for the curvy cart." Crimson shuddered at the memory of her ride on that infernal contraption, but before she could warn Ayla, the elf stood and embraced Crimson. "Silly me, I forgot to ask; will you be my bridesmaid? Say yes, please, please, please."

"You don't need to beg! Of course I'll be your bridesmaid." Crimson's face split into a genuine smile.

"Oooo," Ayla squealed, causing everyone in the café to stare at them. "This is going to be so much fun. I can't wait to see what you come up with for the lobster do!" *What in the queendom was a lobster do?* "You can help me and Jojo plan the wedding. Our first meeting is tomorrow at ten. We'll come to your shop."

Crimson kept the smile on her face as her friend waltzed out of the Cozy Lobster before she collapsed back into her seat. Being Ayla's bridesmaid was one thing, something they'd talked about in vague terms as they planned dream weddings over a shared cup of hot chocolate on their rare days off together back in Oasis. But planning a wedding with the maire. She shuddered. What had she signed up for?

Chapter 3

~ *The planning meeting* ~

CRIMSON MASSAGED HER TEMPLES in small circles as the maire continued to wax lyrical about all the native flowers in Saffron Vale.

"…and, naturally, we'll want to ensure that there are saffron poppies in the posies. They're rare, but I hear that Ignatius has had success growing some out near his lighthouse."

"No saffron poppies." Crimson raised her voice. She had had an unpleasant experience collecting those poppy heads for Ig, almost falling asleep on the side of the mountain. If it hadn't been for a bad-tempered sheep, she might still be there.

"It's our proud vale's second most known flower, after the crocus, of course." The maire frowned.

"It makes people drowsy. You don't want anyone falling

asleep at the wedding."

The maire tapped a finger to his chin. "There is that consideration…but still…"

"Jojo, we want people awake. I think the crocuses will be perfect. If they're half as beautiful as the pictures you've shown me, it will be perfect."

"They are half as beautiful as you, my honeybunch."

Ayla giggled and reached for the maire's hand, and he leaned in for a kiss. Crimson scribbled in her new notebook, keeping her gaze firmly off the couple, as they finally made a decision on the flowers. Next to her, Hardy, the town clerk, studied his own papers.

"With sunflowers, of course," Ayla said, once she had finished with her fiancé's lips.

"I'm not sure sunflowers will be the easiest to mix in with crocuses…" Crimson tried.

The maire waved his fingers at her. "Nonsense, you will find a way. Now, we should discuss cake…"

And so it went on. Both of them spurring each other to more absurd heights as Crimson took notes in the notebook she had bought for this express purpose. She sighed and crossed through the plain sponge idea as the maire rambled on about saffron cake and chocolate ganache, a combination which made Crimson purse her lips, not sure how the fruit cake with its subtle sweet flavour would fare against rich chocolate.

On a cue from the maire, Hardy handed her a sketch on a

napkin. Crimson recognised Maire Bowan's scrawls. Extravagant would be an understatement. The drawing was a twelve-tier monstrosity with writing that said things like 'swirly bits here' and 'embellishments'. *At least he had a vision.* Crimson almost laughed to stop herself from crying at the absurdity of it all.

Crimson took a deep breath. "And are you making the cake, Ayla?"

Her friend laughed. The maire shook his head. "No, no, no. That won't do. My Ayay might be the most talented baker in the queendom, but she cannot work on her wedding day. Fie, Miss Brouderer, you should know better. No, we shall ask the proprietor of the Cozy Lobster to create a confection worthy of our nuptials. Money is no object."

"OK." Crimson wrote that down, wondering what Dilly would have to say about the matter. "Now, what about the guest list." Dilly would need to know numbers for the cake.

Hardy passed her a wad of paper without saying a word. Three pages of names. Front and back. Three columns per page. In tiny writing.

"We're keeping it small," said the maire.

Crimson studied his face. He smiled back at her with no sign that this was a joke. Maybe a satyr's idea of small was to invite everyone he'd ever met.

"And my family," added Ayla.

Hardy dug through his sheaf and found another, smaller, list of names.

"So how many in total?"

"Four hundred and eighty-seven," said Hardy.

Crimson dropped her quill.

The maire sniffed. "That's an odd number, maybe we should round it up to an even five hundred. I haven't invited my chums from the supper club." He nodded. "Yes. Five hundred it is."

"Five hundred," Crimson repeated the number, hoping she'd misheard.

Hardy shot Crimson a sympathetic look.

The maire nodded, then checked his pocket watch. "Now, I'm afraid I must away my love, there's a planning meeting happening in less than half an hour and if we don't get there early, all the chocolate biscuits will be gone."

Ayla patted his round belly with a smile. "Not a problem, Jojo, I want to discuss my dress with Crimson, anyway."

Crimson buried her head in her notebook again as they shared an amorous parting that bordered on indecent and then she was alone with her best friend.

"Are you sure?"

Ayla frowned, and her button nose crinkled in confusion.

"About all this, I mean," Crimson clarified. She had just about come to terms with her friend's choice of partner, but this wedding bordered on obscene. The size alone meant that it rivalled some of Queen Liana's parties.

"Oh yes." Ayla sighed happily. "I want everyone to know how much I love Jojo."

Crimson narrowed her eyes. *Had Ayla taken a love potion?* Because the sappy elf sitting in front of her sounded nothing like her best friend. She'd have to check with Dilly. The petalborn knew a thing or two about brewing love teas.

"But enough about the guest list. I want to talk about the dress."

Crimson smiled. Designing dresses was both a career and a joy and she could talk about fabrics and patterns for hours. She pulled her design book towards her and flipped it to a blank page. A hundred ideas flitted through her mind. She'd sketched some of them down last night, but the most important rule of bespoke dresses was that the customer was happy.

So, she didn't share any of her drawings with Ayla and instead asked, "What sort of things do you love?"

"In a dress?"

"You can go broader than clothing. What's your vision for your look? What do you want people to think when they see you?"

"I don't care what anyone thinks, except for Jojo. I just want him to look at me as if I'm the most beautiful elf in the queendom and I want him to think 'wow'."

Crimson wrote down 'wow' in capital letters.

"But other than that, do what you want. I trust you."

Crimson blinked at her design book. "But I need to know more. Do you want a train? What about the neckline?"

Ayla placed her hand over Crimson's. "I trust you. You're brilliant."

Crimson swallowed, tears filling her eyes. Ayla's faith in her was too much. "What if I create something you hate?"

"You won't. You know me. Now how about some more tea?" With that, her friend stood and made her way to the kitchen, bustling about as if she owned the place. Ayla always was confident in a kitchen. If Crimson didn't stop her, she'd probably whip up some biscuits to go with the tea. Although, where she'd find the ingredients in Crimson's kitchen was a mystery. Crimson and cooking went together like sand and lacy undergarments. Not at all.

Chapter 4

~ To be a teg ~

ONCE AYLA HAD LEFT, Crimson massaged her temples and ran through her notebook. There was so much to do. Her gaze strayed to the framed certificate hung on the wall behind the counter. She was a guilder, now. Pride surged through her and Crimson stood a little taller. She was a guilder of the Dressmakers' Guild. And she would rise to meet any challenge thrown her way.

This was nothing trickier than trying out a complex pattern design for the first time; you arranged all the pieces, read the instructions – twice, measured, cut, pinned, made a toile – a mock-up of the garment out of inexpensive plain fabric, all before you started on the main event.

Preparation was the key.

So, how could she prepare for a wedding?

A list!

She could turn the convoluted ideas that Ayla and the maire had into practical steps that might actually be achievable. Then she'd have a clear idea of what needed to be done, by when. Planning a wedding might seem overwhelming, but if she could sew with slippery silk without stretching the fabric, she could do anything. If she approached it like a complicated sewing project, then she had half a chance of meeting the couple's high expectations.

Crimson flipped her wedding notebook to the back page to start her list on a fresh sheet. If only she were a full-blooded teg, then she could wish this wedding into being.

Crimson paused and reached for the latest letter from her teggish correspondent. They had started writing to each other after she'd helped him in the street and he'd recognised her face from the papers. Their first letters had stayed polite, but Crimson couldn't resist asking for details about tegs.

Tegs were a shy folk, not many of them chose to make their home in the queendom and still fewer in the larger cities and towns, like Oasis where Crimson had grown up. Crimson's mother was an exception, someone who'd stayed in the town, kept her head down and earned enough respect that when she passed away, the Dressmakers' Guild had apprenticed Crimson to one of their guilders.

Part of this shyness was due to prejudices against tegs. Everyone knew the stories; tegs were tricksy, never bargain with a teg because they'll always get the better end of the deal.

The tales said that tegs had wish magic, but any wishes granted came true in the worst ways. If someone asked for fame, it was more likely to come from a journalist happening to witness an embarrassing moment and writing it up than what they truly wanted. And someone wishing for a long life might find their loved ones passing away before them.

Crimson had spent many lonely nights as an apprentice wishing for things that never came true. At least, not until she took a chance and moved to Saffron Vale.

As Crimson had come to learn through the letters, tegs did indeed have wish magic, but they rarely chose to grant wishes and had no control over the outcome. So, if someone thought their wish had turned out wrong, the tegs couldn't change it, but they still got the blame. Which was why they chose to live apart in another plane, one only tegs could access. Crimson didn't understand much about it, but accessing the aether was the source of the tegs' magic, much like any other magical being.

She scanned the latest letter for the fiftieth time.

Dear Crimson (they had long moved past using formal titles)

I read your last letter with great pleasure, you have no idea how lovely it is to read about your success, and I even saw someone wearing one of your 'pocket' dresses in Capital City. The bright colours and contrasting pockets made me sure it was one of yours.

You asked about our wish magic in your last letter. We can grant wishes. There. Now you know; the stories are true. But they are not true in other respects; we do not ask for impossible bargains in exchange for the wishes, and we do not take pleasure when things don't work out.

Perhaps an ancestor, some teg back in long forgotten days, delighted in playing tricks on people and granted wishes without thinking of the consequences. Perhaps they used their magic for selfish gain. Or perhaps they were so powerful they could contravene the limitations on usual teg magic; no bringing people back to life and no making people fall in love with you (lust is a different matter entirely!). Who knows what happened in the past?

But we have learned the hard way not to meddle with others' lives. People think they know what they want, but it is so often not what they need. And they wish for fame, or money, or love without wanting to put in the effort to get there.

That's the true secret to granting wishes, Crimson; know what you really want and work hard to get there. Take advantage of opportunities that come your way, of course, like you did with the competition, but your success is a result of your own talent and hard work.

You asked if a half-teg might have some vestige of wish magic. I do not know. You are a rarity in the queendom as not many of us choose to live outside of our home plane nowadays. Your mother was always exceptional in that regard. If you have not noticed that you can grant wishes, have not experienced the tingle of magic flowing through your veins, then I think perhaps not. But perhaps it is because you have not yet accessed the aether.

Wishing you all the best, your friend,

Artor Voeux

Accessing the aether…how on earth did one go about that? Crimson shook her head. Other magicals might know, but Guilder Senda had drilled into her that it wasn't polite to ask people if they could do magic. He had preferred to pretend it didn't exist. She would just have to write back and ask if he had any tips on making a connection with the aether plane.

A spark of silver in one of the corners where the ceiling met the walls caught her eye. She smiled as she saw the small luck spider that had chosen to live with her making its way across her web.

"Perhaps you can grant me the luck I need to make this wedding the best ever for Ayla." Crimson waited a beat. Sometimes the spider wrote words in the gossamer strands of her web. At least, they looked like words. Crimson chose to believe that the tiny arachnid looked out for her and helped her. But, no words appeared today.

With a sigh, Crimson dashed off a letter to her teggish friend before moving back to the wedding list of jobs to do.

Chapter 5

~ *The theme is decided* ~

CRIMSON SIPPED HER TEA to prevent her mouth from saying something she would regret. Ayla and the maire – she still couldn't quite bring herself to call him by his first name – sat at her table at yet another planning meeting discussing everything about the wedding without making a decision on anything.

"We must have a clear link to Saffron Vales, m'dear," Maire Bowan said with a smile, gesturing at his embroidered waistcoat which featured crocuses set off against a green background.

"Yes, this is such a quaint vale," Ayla agreed, rolling a crumb of golden saffron cake between her fingers.

"Quaint! It is innovative," the maire banged his hand on the table, causing the cake to jump off its plate, "we are the premier vale for dyeing and fabric weaving in the queendom and one of the richest to boot."

Ayla looked down at her hands, then back up, eyes wide and lashes fluttering. "Have we just had our first fight?"

Crimson drank more tea.

"I think you're quite right, and we must celebrate our reunion post haste. Miss Brouderer, you can work on the finer details, can't you? While me and my fiancée here rekindle our passion for one another…" The maire kissed up and down Ayla's slender arm with loud squelching noises. Ayla giggled, but she didn't pull away.

Crimson put down her cup with enough force that it made them both look at her. Any more to drink and she would have to leave to use the privy and goodness knows what they'd get up to in her kitchen. "You haven't decided on anything."

Both Ayla and the maire blinked at her.

"You need a theme before we can decide anything else," Crimson said, a hint of exasperation creeping into her voice.

"A theme…" the maire repeated.

"Something that ties everything together, so it doesn't look like a hodge podge of ideas."

"How about 'Saffron Vale'?" Maire Bowan raised his hands as if he was drawing a sign.

Ayla clapped. "I love it. And we can have sunflowers, they're yellow."

"Excellent idea, my love. And crocuses. And saffron poppies. And…" the maire's brow furrowed as he thought, "…lobsters!"

"Lobsters!" Crimson rubbed her temples, feeling a headache coming on.

Maire Bowan sniffed. "The Great Lobster is the emblem of our vale. Which reminds me, I must invite them to the wedding."

Crimson groaned and added 'Great Lobster' to the guest list. At some point they would have to stop adding people and actually send invites, and then they could sort the catering. And the venue. Crimson's head rang with all the things that needed to be done.

"You still haven't introduced me to them. When can we see them?" Ayla asked, oblivious to the growing to do list.

"Now, now, dear, while I am a personal friend of the old Lobby, they keep to their own time. But you shall definitely see them at the harvest, and I shall issue an invitation to our wedding personally."

"So your theme is 'Saffron Vale' and your colours are…"

"Yellow," said Ayla decisively.

"And purple, for the crocuses." Maire Bowan smiled.

Crimson smiled, approving of the bold colour choices. Some people might think that purple and yellow clashed, but in the right hues, they could look elegant, regal even.

"Well, now we have a theme, we'll leave you to it, Miss

Brouderer. My fiancée and I have a fight to make up for…"

"Hello, hello, hello!" The shop bell tinkled, announcing a customer.

Crimson got to her feet and raced to the shop. Didn't people read? She had turned the painted wooden sign to 'closed'. "I'm terribly sorry, but we're closed for the morning for a friend's wedding." Her lips turned up as she saw a tall, curved felinix standing in the middle of the shop with one hand on their hip and the other thrust towards the ceiling in a pose.

Chapter 6

~ The entertainment has arrived ~

"**S**IBBY!"

The famous felinix stepped forward and embraced Crimson, pulling her against their golden rosetted fur and planting a fake kiss on each of Crimson's cheeks with a loud 'mwah' noise.

"Darrrling," Sibby purred, rolling the r's in their deep voice as if they were talking to a lover, "the entertainment has arrived. I am here for the wedding."

"Sibby, you old cat, you came!" Maire Bowan beamed at her from the doorway.

"Less of the old," Sibby ran a hand down their furred cheek, "I pay good money to look this young. And of course, I came, you silly goat. I wouldn't miss such a big event in my home vale, and the amount you're paying me for the entertainment will help me keep these youthful looks." They shot a wink at the maire.

"Ayla, Miss Brouderer, allow me the honour of introducing you to our home star hero, Sibby."

"We've met." Crimson took some pleasure in seeing the wind taken out of Maire Bowan's sails at her pronouncement.

"I saw you in the Capital. Your show is amazing!" Ayla gushed.

"Always nice to meet a fan." Sibby took Ayla's hand and pulled her in to give her an air kiss on each cheek.

"I can't believe you can jump into the splits like that. How do you do it?"

"Practice, darrling. And a lot of tinctures that relive the pain. Now, I was told that I would get a Brouderer original to perform in." Sibby arched an eyebrow at Crimson.

"Were you now?" Crimson turned to the maire and folded her arms.

"Of course, that way you can make sure it fits with the theme. Now, we'll leave you to sort the details, unless you want us to stay for the fitting." The maire waggled his eyebrows at Sibby.

"A lady likes to keep some secrets, Bowan."

"But you're no lady, Sibby."

"Ain't that the truth." They both burst into laughter and Crimson felt her body loosen and her face relax into a smile as the maire threw his head back and roared his amusement. *Satyr magic.* The words whispered through her mind. She'd experienced some of the maire's magic at the celebration party for her guild membership, and she didn't like the thought of being out of control of her actions or emotions.

Get it together, Brouderer. As quickly as the burst of amusement had come, it left, and Crimson pursed her lips.

"We'll leave you to it, then." With that, the maire led Ayla out, leaving Crimson alone with Sibby.

The felinix prowled around the shop, plucking at shimmering fabrics and shining ribbons. "I hear you're a guilder now. Congratulations."

"Thank you." A warm sensation flushed through Crimson's entire body. She would never get used to the pleasure of being a guilder. It brought her a legitimacy and certain protections and privileges with ATOZ, the queendom's premier trading company, but most of all it told her that she belonged somewhere, that she had a tribe in a world where she had felt so alone for most of her life, and that was worth the long apprenticeship and the trials of competition, and even the betrayal of her friend.

"So," Sibby folded herself gracefully into the overstuffed chair that Crimson had in a corner for her clients, "what did you have in mind for the star of the wedding?"

"Isn't the star of the wedding the bride?"

Sibby waved an arm. "Darrling, if I'm in the wedding, I'm

the star.”

“To be honest, this is the first I've heard of designing you a dress. I didn't know you were part of the wedding.” In her head, Crimson added Sibby to the ever-growing guest list.

Sibby arched a perfect eyebrow. “Well, I wasn't sure I could take time out of my schedule. But, this is going to be the wedding of the year, so how could I refuse? What's the theme?”

“Saffron Vale.”

Sibby rolled her eyes. “Not original, but it fits, I suppose. I'll need at least three outfits…” They tapped a claw against the arm of the chair.

“Three?” Crimson sank against the countertop. When would she have time to make three outfits plus a wedding dress?

Sibby waved away her concerns. “I'll dig two out of my costumes, but I want you to make my showstopper dress. Beading, jewels, big skirts, a reveal.” Sibby ticked each item off on their long fingers, stopped and studied Crimson's confused face. “Have you seen one of my shows?”

Crimson shook her head, too stunned to reply.

“Then you simply must come to one, darrling. I'm putting a small soiree on tomorrow evening at the Salt and Pickle Inn. It's not exactly a Capital City theatre, but I like to give a bit back to the community while I'm in town. I'll leave you two tickets at the door. Bring whoever you like. Now, how do you want to take my measurements?” Sibby unfolded her long legs and stood.

"Er, in my workroom. Upstairs."

Sibby strode off and Crimson grabbed her design book and a pencil and hurried after the glamourous felinix. "It's nice of you to come here when you're so busy. Where are you going after this?" Crimson skidded to a halt as she entered the workroom to find Sibby already stripped to their undergarments. The felinix didn't waste any time.

Sibby's brow puckered the tiniest amount. "I'm not going anywhere."

Crimson gestured to the rose-coloured dress that lay discarded on the bed. It was the sort of garment that spoke of an evening out on the town, perhaps fine dining or dancing.

Sibby laughed. "That old thing? I wear that to wash the dishes, darrling. A little glamour every day is important, don't you agree?"

Crimson smiled at the felinix's infectious joy and took out her measuring tape. She could judge Sibby's size by eye, but for bespoke gowns it was better to double check. "You have a perfect hourglass figure." Crimson couldn't help the compliment that slipped from her mouth. "Sorry." *Inappropriate.* Guilder Senda's voice hissed through her mind, still reprimanding her after two years away from his shop.

"Never apologise, darrling. Not for anything and certainly not for a compliment. I never do. And it's all mine."

Crimson raised her eyebrows at the blatant lie. Without Sibby's dress on, the layers of corsetry and padding were obvious.

Sibby gave her a wink. "One hundred per cent mine. After all, I paid for it."

Crimson laughed at that and finished the measurements.

"Remember to add six inches for the shoes."

Crimson leaned back on her heels and looked up at the tall felinix. "Six inches? How can you walk in those?"

"Come to the show tomorrow and you'll see what I can do with six-inch heels." Sibby gave her a suggestive look and her tail crooked into a question mark. Crimson laughed. Did Sibby ever switch off the sassy persona they wore like armour?

"You can be yourself here, you know. Don't feel like you have to perform for me." Crimson stood up and wrote the final figures into her book.

"Life is a performance, darrling." Sibby gave her a sympathetic look, as if Crimson hadn't learned an important life lesson. "We are who we present to the world. Good or bad, our actions define us, and I choose how I'm defined."

"Sorry."

Sibby chucked Crimson under the chin. "Never apologise. And never live your life for someone else. If you want something, take it. Grab it by the balls."

"What?"

"Life!" Sibby stepped into her dress and pulled it up, shimmying into the sparkling fabric. "See you at the show." Sibby left in a whirlwind of air kisses and fur and Crimson sank onto her bed.

This was too much. It was all too much. A wedding dress was a big enough task, and now she had another dress to design. One with beading and a reveal, whatever that meant. With the same deadline. This was an impossible commission. A commission impossible. The words swirled in her head until she was dizzy.

Smudge leapt up onto the bed, jumping on her stomach with unerring accuracy before hopping off. He repeated that five times until Crimson sat up. "Fine. Let's go for a walk."

Chapter 7

~ *A misunderstanding* ~

SOMEONE'S FABRIC HAD ESCAPED from the dyeing pools further upstream. Such a shame. All that wasted fabric. It wasn't hers, was it? Ig had promised her white fabric, and that material was white. But he wouldn't use the dyeing pools for white, would he?

Crimson hurried forwards. The only way to be sure was to get to Ig's pool and see if there was material safely soaking in whatever dye he was experimenting with this week. She followed the path, getting closer to the river, until the fabric took on a shape under the flowing water.

It looked like a dress. Crimson breathed more easily. People dyed fabric before it was made into clothes, not after. At least, that was the traditional way. Crimson pushed that thought aside for now, because it was odd that someone's clothes would get swept away. She walked closer.

Wait. Was that someone in the river?

Crimson sprinted to the riverbank. Dark hair snaked through the water like ribbons. Someone was in trouble.

Crimson kicked off her pine green boots and dived into the river without a second thought. She waded out, the river mud sucking at her feet and clouding the crystal-clear water. And then it was too deep to wade; her chin barely came above the surface of the water and Crimson cursed her teggish ancestry for making her so tiny.

She stopped straining for the river bottom and paddled out to where the person floated beneath the surface, wishing she were a stronger swimmer. But Guilder Senda – her former mentor – hadn't deemed swimming an essential skill for his apprentices. The only experience she had with water was a few lazy days splashing in a nearby lake on the occasions that she was allowed to tag along with Guilder Senda's family on their rare time away from the shop.

Something slithered past her legs. Crimson screamed and ducked under the water in panic. What sort of slimy monsters lived in this river? A flash of rainbow scales darted towards her, and something nudged her back above the surface. She looked for her rescuer and murmured "thank you" at a flash of a multicoloured tail.

On the bank, Smudge hopped up and down, whining before jumping in. Crimson shouted at him to 'stay', but he was already swimming over to her with powerful strokes befitting a coastal dragon. At least one of them was comfortable in the water.

She struck out again and reached the person drifting in the current. Crimson sucked in a breath and dived, reaching out, unable to see in the water dirtied by her floundering.

Her hand found skin and Crimson pulled, putting all her strength into dragging this person to the surface. The body jerked at her contact. Crimson gasped at the sudden movement, letting out all the air in her lungs.

Smudge swam around her in elegant circles. This was all a game to him.

Confused, Crimson felt around frantically for the body while her lungs burned. She kicked for the surface. But the water was so murky. Which way was up? Her feet tangled in her cumbersome dress. Why hadn't she taken it off before she dived in? Now she was going to die in the river next to the person she couldn't save.

Light. A chink of sunshine through the clouds of muck in the river and a surge of hope gave Crimson renewed strength. One final burst. Crimson moved her arms and legs as her body weakened. Just a little further.

Too far. Just out of reach. Her lungs burned. She opened her mouth to take a breath. Freezing, dirty water filled her throat. She coughed, convulsing as the water got into her lungs. Stars swam in front of her eyes.

Strong hands grabbed her and pulled her up. Coughing and

spluttering, Crimson pushed at the unknown attacker, confused and scared, knowing only that she would die.

"It's me. Stop fighting," a sweet voice panted.

Ovelia.

Crimson stopped struggling and allowed the dwarf to pull her to the riverbank.

"What were you thinking?"

Crimson collapsed to the ground and bent over her knees, hacking and coughing up mucky river water. When she was done, she lay on her back, savouring the cool breaths of air. In and out. Breathing was amazing. How could people go through their lives without thinking about it? In and out. Her lungs sang with the joy of it, wanting more. Her chest moved faster.

"Calm down or you'll hyperventilate." Ovelia's voice cut through Crimson's contemplation.

Smudge clambered out and shook water from his back, sending a cascade of droplets over her

Crimson forced herself to take slow, deep breaths, feeling her lungs expand to their fullest with each inhalation. After three exhales, she turned to her saviour. Why was Ovelia in the river wearing her clothes? "Are you alright? I thought you had drowned."

Ovelia snorted. "Not likely."

"Then what were you doing in the river?"

"Practicing."

Crimson blinked. "You weren't moving." Cold rushed through her body. She had almost died. Her teeth chattered, her hands trembled, and the shaking made its way through her body until she shook like a leaf caught in a summer's breeze. Smudge nudged her hands, and his warm scales felt like burning fire on her skin.

"Come on, we'd better get you somewhere warm."

Chapter 8

~ *Awkwardness in a cabin* ~

OVELIA HAULED CRIMSON TO her feet and wrapped a strong arm around her waist. "Come on, one foot in front of the other."

Crimson trudged along beside the dwarf, her head swirling while Smudge raced ahead. What had Ovelia meant by 'practicing'? Several times, she tried to form the question, but the words wouldn't flow through her trembling lips. And it was cold. So cold. Her skin pricked into goosebumps and her dress weighed her down, dripping water in a trail behind them.

Crimson didn't even recognise the path until Ovelia turned off down a path to a log house. She froze.

"N-no." Crimson managed to whisper the word. Her voice didn't want to come out any louder.

"It's the closest place, and Lief'll know what to do."

Crimson pulled back. She had avoided Lief for months, scurrying away any time he'd tried to speak to her. And that was ruddy difficult to do in such a small place, so she wasn't about to ruin her streak by knocking on his door. "T-town."

"That's too far. You're in shock and possibly on your way to hypothermia." Ovelia shook her head. "What were you thinking?"

Crimson stared at the dwarf. "Next t-time I won't bother saving you."

Ovelia laughed. "I think you'll recover. But we have to get you warm." She ushered Crimson up the path to the door before banging on it several times.

Crimson stared at the grain of one of the logs, tracing its curving pattern with her gaze. Maybe he wouldn't be in.

The door opened to reveal Lief's scarred face. He looked the two soaking women up and down. "Been river swimming?"

Ovelia nodded. "She's in shock." She jerked a thumb at Crimson.

"I'm f-fine."

"You sound it," said Lief. "Come in."

Crimson shook her head. "F-fine," she repeated. If she said it enough times, maybe it would be true.

Smudge darted through the door.

Lief sighed, stepped forward and picked her up as if she weighed nothing. He carried her inside and set her down on the soft rug in the front room.

Crimson hugged her knees to her chest. How humiliating. She glared up at Lief.

"You need to take off that dress," he said.

Crimson flushed, suddenly hot and embarrassed despite the chill that flowed through her. The last time he'd seen her in her underwear, he'd run out on her in the morning to breakfast with another woman.

"Stop scaring her."

Crimson snapped her head up at the throaty female voice. The voice that belonged to the woman who had accompanied him back from Innton. She hugged her knees tighter.

Lief glared at the woman. "She needs to get warm and she can't do that in soaking clothes."

Ovelia didn't have the same modesty as Crimson and tugged her wet, almost transparent undergarments off, wrapping herself in a blanket.

"Here." The unfamiliar woman handed Crimson a woollen blanket. Crimson couldn't move her hand to take it. This was the person Lief had chosen over her. Mistaking Crimson's silence for shyness, the woman carried on talking. "I'm Bircha. Don't worry about him; he's all bark, no bite."

Lief huffed, turned his back and put another log on the small fire that cheered the room.

Crimson took the covering and held it around herself as she shrugged off her dress in an awkward dance.

"Give that here." Bircha took the soggy dress and hung it on an airer with Ovelia's underdress. "Now you two sit there while I make a restorative drink."

The smell of cinnamon and apples soon filled the log house and Crimson sat next to Ovelia, careful to keep herself covered. She traced the faded tartan with a finger. It was worn, but comfortable, with none of the itchiness that came from coarse wool; the sign of a well-made cloth.

From the safety of the low sofa, Crimson studied her rival. She shook her head. *Where had that thought come from?* There was no rivalry. Lief wasn't a prize to be won, and he had made his choice clear. And who could blame him? Bircha was gorgeous; tall, dark haired with dark eyes and tanned skin that spoke of outside living. She matched Lief to a tee. Even their clothes matched. Bircha wore fitted trousers under a skirt that came to her knees and a loose, plain top. It wasn't fussy or fashionable and it suited her well. Her and Lief made a good pair. *So, move on.*

Crimson turned to Ovelia, who lounged in her blanket towel. "What were you practicing for?"

For the first time since entering Lief's house, Ovelia looked uncomfortable. She shifted on the sofa and plucked at the cloth covering her. "For leaving."

"You're going somewhere?"

Ovelia sighed. "We have to."

"I'm not following."

"I didn't ask you to."

Both women looked at each other, their brows knitting in confusion.

Crimson closed her eyes to gather her patience and pushed a sodden lock of hair away from her face. "I'm not following the conversation."

"Me and Hamlet. We're leaving Saffron Vale. It's the only way we'll be together."

"And you're planning to swim upstream?"

Ovelia snorted a desperate laugh. "No. But our parents will follow us, so we're going to fake our deaths."

"Wouldn't a sleeping draught be easier?" Bircha handed them a shot glass filled with a thick, green liquid before retreating to the kitchen area.

Ovelia downed hers in one and sucked in a breath while slapping her knee.

"Don't give them ideas." Crimson sniffed the liquid, her nose wrinkling at the strong medicinal scent.

Bircha returned with two mugs of mulled cider. She handed one to Ovelia but held Crimson's out of reach. "Not until you've drunk that. It'll warm you."

The spicy drink lit her tongue on fire. Crimson spluttered but managed to swallow the shot down. "This is almost as bad as the hangover cure."

Bircha laughed. "He told me about that. Scrumpy hangovers are the worst. And this uses some of the same herbs. They're medicinal." If that meant they tasted awful, Crimson agreed. "Here." Bircha handed over the mug of cider.

Crimson took it and stared at the cloudy liquid as her cheeks heated – whether from the shot of that awful drink or embarrassment, she didn't know. How dare Lief share private details of her hangover with this stranger? Wasn't there such a thing as hangover confidentiality? If there wasn't, there should be.

Crimson cupped her freezing hands around the warm mug, letting the heat of the drink course through her skin and the homely scent of spiced apple surround her. Bircha could cook too. *Was there anything the woman couldn't do?*

"We thought of sleeping potions," said Ovelia. "But there's a lot that can go wrong. You've heard the Ballad of Omeo and Hughliette."

Bircha nodded. The ballad was well-known throughout the queendom and considered a tragic romance and a warning to both young lovers and overprotective families.

"We haven't got a choice," Ovelia wailed. "You saw Dad and Hamlet's mum the other day. They can't even be in the same room together; there's no way they'll allow us to be together and I'm tired of sneaking around. It was fun at first, but now it feels wrong. Why should I have to hide my love for him? It's not fair."

"You shouldn't have to hide your feelings about anyone." Lief prodded the fire with a poker and stood.

Crimson met his gaze and turned away, sipping the mulled

cider. She had thought they had feelings for each other and now he was apparently living with someone else, and she was stuck here until she could get some dry clothes. She turned her attention back to Ovelia's problem. "I think if someone sits down and explains things to your parents, they'll see sense. They're reasonable people."

Ovelia pulled her into a hug. "Oh, thank you, Crimson. They'll listen to you. They have to."

"What?"

"When do you want me to set up a meeting?"

"Meeting?" Crimson echoed weakly.

"You said you'd speak to Dad and Hamlet's mum for us. Don't worry, I'll sort something out. Thank you."

"I said someone should speak to them," Crimson mumbled. Ovelia didn't hear but both Lief and Bircha's mouths twitched. They were so in sync, it was sickening. Crimson couldn't stay a moment longer in this house. She stood and pulled her blanket around her body.

"I should go."

"But your clothes–"

"Will dry well enough at home."

"At least let me lend you something to wear."

Crimson wanted to refuse Bircha's offer, but the woman was too darned nice. She followed the dark-haired beauty to a bedroom and looked around while Bircha dug in a sack. So, this was Lief's room.

Crimson's gaze wandered to the bed, made up with thick covers layered over each other to give a cosy feel with a thick knitted quilt over the top that had frayed ends. Her fingers itched to fix it; a quick blanket stitch round the edge or a lining under the knitting would prolong its life. But then she remembered that she wasn't friends – or anything – with Lief anymore.

"Here. It's a bit big, but it'll do. You're lucky you're so tiny; I always wished I wasn't so tall or so thick about the hips." Bircha gave her a lopsided grin.

"Thank you." Crimson took the shirt and pressed her lips together. It was her teggish ancestry that made her so small, not anything she could choose. If anything, she'd rather have a curvier figure, like Bircha's generously proportioned frame.

"Are you sure you won't stay and wait? We can start a game of Bread and Butter."

"I should get back. Smudge doesn't do well away from the house for so long."

Bircha looked into the other room where the small dragon rolled over so Lief could rub his belly. "Really?"

"If you could give me a minute."

"Of course, I forget not everyone's as comfortable with nakedness as me and Lief." Bircha shut the door behind her on her way out.

Crimson stared at the closed door for a long moment. *'Comfortable with nakedness', indeed.* Could the woman be any more brazen? With a shake of her head, Crimson dropped the blanket and changed, tucking the oversized shirt into the too-long trousers. Dressed, she retrieved her boots and prised Smudge away from Lief before leaving.

Chapter 9

~ Crimson tries her hand at matchmaking ~

THE FOLLOWING EVENING SAW Crimson at the Salt and Pickle Inn in the centre of Woolton along with the majority of the Saffron Vale residents.

Ig perused the flier with interest as they queued. "I wonder why it's called the *Scrumpy Tour?*"

"No idea," said Crimson, smiling at people she recognised in the crowd.

Ayla waved back at her before leaning down so that the maire could whisper in her pointed ear. Crimson looked away, only to see Lief and Bircha standing towards the back of the queue, towering over Ovelia, who strained her neck talking to them. Crimson smiled, then sighed. That was another thing she needed to do; talk to Ovelia and Hamlet's parents.

Lief met her gaze and gave her a crooked smile. Crimson turned her back on him. How dare he smile at her?

"Do you think it means there will be apples?" Ig asked, still studying the leaflet in his hands. "Or will there be scrumpy served there?"

Crimson shuddered. "Don't talk to me about scrumpy." The last time she'd had the deceptive apple alcohol, she'd had the mother of all hangovers. And worse, had woken up at Lief's house. Back when she'd thought he still cared for her.

Coming here was a bad idea. She opened her mouth to tell Ig that she'd changed her mind when the tylluan gripped her hand tight.

"He's here." Ig gave a nervous hoot. Crimson turned her head. "Don't look!"

She smiled at her friend, who peered over her shoulder with his huge eyes. "Alright. You can look now. No!" Crimson snapped her head back and gave Ig a look. "Now. Don't make it obvious."

Crimson rotated slowly on the spot, like she was taking in the crowd. When she saw Milus, the minotaur blacksmith, she waggled her fingers at him. He smiled back, returned her wave with his metallic hand and started walking towards them.

At her side, Ig gave another anxious hoot. "Why is he coming over? I'm not prepared." He got out a notebook from one of his many pockets.

Crimson placed a hand over his and smoothed down his fluffed-up feathers. "It's alright. Maybe this is a good thing. You can talk, enjoy the show together. In fact, maybe I should leave you two alone…"

Ig's eyes widened as his anxiety turned to full-blown panic, and he grabbed Crimson's hands. "Do not leave me. Oh, good evening, Milus. I didn't see you there."

"Evening," the minotaur said, inclining his head. He rocked back and forth on his feet, but didn't have anything else to say.

Crimson tried to fill the gap. They were just as bad as each other when it came to shyness. "Well, this is quite the event."

"Yarp," agreed Milus.

Ig nodded and his fingers opened and closed around his notebook, his back as straight as a pole.

Crimson searched for another topic of conversation. "How's the blacksmithing business?"

"Can't complain."

That shut down that avenue then. She peered through the crowd. "When do you think they'll open the doors?"

"When they're ready, I expect."

Crimson shot Milus a side eye. Was that a joke? But the minotaur's face remained impassive. A bead of sweat ran down his bull's head and the fingers on his good hand twitched.

"Now that's an interesting concept." Ig coughed.

"Readiness, I mean. I've read that one way to get people more interested in something is to keep them waiting. The pleasure is in the anticipation, so to speak. I wonder if Sibby has studied the human condition at all because everyone seems eager enough. See how people lean forward and keep turning to the doors. Eager."

Oh no, now Ig was rambling. Milus tilted his head to one side politely.

How could she save Ig from totally embarrassing himself? The wedding bubbled to the top of Crimson's mind. Maybe Milus could help with one of her many to do list items. "I've been meaning to talk to you, Milus."

The minotaur tilted his head to the other side, dragging his cow-eyed gaze from the tylluan's face. Crimson took that as a sign to keep talking. "The maire and Ayla need rings to exchange, and I thought it would be lovely if we could source as much as possible from Saffron Vale. It's important to both of them."

"Yarp." Milus' brow crinkled. "But I don't take your meaning."

Crimson gave him a bright smile. "What if you made the rings?"

Milus gave two slow blinks and then shook his enormous head, his horns catching the light from the windows of the inn. "I'm a blacksmith, not a jeweller. Ignatius is better at more delicate work than I am."

Was that a hint of tenderness in the minotaur's gaze? Crimson's smile spread. They were perfect for each other. "Ig? Is that true?" Crimson knew that Ig's curiosity meant he dabbled in all sorts of fields of study and invention, but ring making as well?

The tylluan shifted on his feet. "I haven't made jewellery, but I'm sure it's not so different to clock making."

Visions of Ayla wearing a cog around her ring finger flashed in front of Crimson's eyes. "It's fine, I'll sort something out." She knew a dwarf in Capital City who might be able to help. Something else to add to her list; *write to dwarf and cash in on favour*. "Oh look, the doors have opened. Sit with us, Milus."

Behind Milus' back, Ig shook his head so fast that his feathers trembled.

Crimson looped her arm through Ig's and patted his hand. "This is not the next stage in the list," Ig hissed at her.

"You don't have to speak, just sit next to him." Crimson could feel the small owl-like man shaking. She sighed. "Or I can sit next to him."

Ig sagged, gave a relieved hoot, and squeezed her hand. "Thank you."

They made their way into the venue. Tables had been set out in a semicircular fan around a makeshift stage, each with a squat candle lighting the table just enough to see other patrons while keeping the light low.

A scarlet curtain hung from a beam, concealing the majority of the stage from view. The atmosphere buzzed like a hive of bees as everyone took their seats. Ig muttered something about using the facilities before bustling off, bumping into several serving staff in neat kirtles and shirts who moved between the tables, taking orders and flitting between the guests and the bar area where a cyclops shook cocktails and poured out frothy beers and, yes, there was the unassuming scrumpy. Crimson scowled at the pottery jug.

"Something the matter, Red?"

Brilliant. She had spent too long looking around and now she saw Lief and Bircha had appeared next to her. "No," Crimson huffed.

"Is this seat taken?" Lief pulled out the chair next to her.

"Yes."

He gave her a wolfish grin and sat down anyway. Crimson thought up a few names to call him. Bircha folded herself into a chair and hailed a server to take their order with a confidence that Crimson envied.

Crimson folded her arms and turned away, aware of the heat of his body, their thighs almost touching in the packed space. She scooted to the other side of her chair, putting as much distance as she could between them. She couldn't even ask him to find another seat because every table was now full with more people crowding around the bar.

"You've been avoiding me," Lief said.

"Can you blame me?" Crimson hissed. There was no way he was going to turn this into her fault.

"Why?"

Crimson spluttered. Was that a serious question? After the way he'd treated her, shacking up with someone else after kissing her like he'd meant it.

"Ladies, gentlemen, queers and queens, and everyone in between, please welcome to the stage…. Sibby!"

Chapter 10

~ *Sibby puts on a show* ~

THE CURTAINS PULLED BACK to reveal the tall felinix posing on the stage in six-inch heels and a red dress shaped like an apple, complete with a stalk and leaf fascinator on top of a giant wig the same golden colour as their fur.

Sibby waved at the packed room. Music started up from somewhere, cutting off any chance Crimson had to reply to Lief. She ignored him and focused on Sibby as they sang, their rich voice filling the room with caramel sounds as they belted out a popular song – *Loving me is easy, loving you is hard* – while sashaying across the stage, their long skirts swishing over the wooden floor.

Sibby finished the tune and stood, nodding at the applause

that followed, thundering up through the inn like a storm. Crimson leaned forward, caught up in the excitement, almost forgetting who she was sitting next to.

"Well, darrlings, that was a little number from the Capital, but I hear that Saffron Vale has its own tunes. Am I right?"

"Yes!" roared the crowd.

"I said, am I right?"

"YES!"

"Alright then." Sibby snapped their fingers and the music started up again into a jaunty tune, almost a sea shanty. As the music swirled into a crescendo, Sibby twirled and their skirt fell to the ground, revealing a smaller dress that accentuated their long legs, which were covered by stockings embroidered with beaded green and red apples that sparkled in the candlelight. So that was a reveal dress.

Crimson strained forward, eager to see how it was done. A ribbon perhaps? Or hook and eye clasps? She gasped as Sibby leapt into the air and landed in a perfect split at the exact beat that marked the end of the song. Crimson stood, along with most of the audience, and clapped and cheered. The maire let out a wolf whistle.

Sibby got to their feet with an elegant move while holding eye contact with the room. "Now, I don't know about all of you, but that worked up a bit of a thirst in me." Sibby walked down from the stage and into the audience, a spotlight formed from a flickerfire lamp in front of an angled mirror in the beams following their every move. They paused at Crimson's table and took a sip of Bircha's water. "Not strong enough, darrling. Not nearly strong enough for my needs."

The audience laughed.

Sibby snapped their fingers, and a server came over with a large jug of scrumpy. The apple fumes made Crimson's eyes water. This was the strong stuff. Sibby took a large swig and wiped their mouth. "Ah, that's better. But I'm still hot…and this is called the Scrumpy Tour, so…" Strains of a folk song about apples rang through the room. Sibby strutted back onto the stage, took another drink and allowed the scrumpy to fall down their chin before lifting the jug aloft and pouring it over themselves while they danced to a song about apple bobbing, complete with moves that made Crimson blush.

Once they'd finished, someone threw Sibby a towel, and they patted their face dry before licking their lips. "Now, I always like to know who I'm performing for…so let's meet a few of you. But remember, keep your hands to yourselves." They paused and shot a wink at the crowd. "Unless you're invited to touch."

Keeping the white towel, Sibby shimmied back into the audience and paused at every table. They started at the maire's table where he sat with Ayla, Hardy, Dilly and Duncan. "And we've got the maire of Saffron Vale himself with us tonight! A round of applause for Maire Bowan."

A polite smattering of claps went up from the room.

"Don't be like that, Saffronians, you voted for him," Sibby

said with a smile that took the sting out of the jibe. The audience laughed. "Now, some say that Maire Bowan is the horniest of maires – pun intended," another wink to the crowd as the maire stroked his small goat horns, "but I've heard it from the goat's mouth himself that he's engaged to be married. Yes, your maire will shortly be off the market for good."

An audible sigh came from somewhere at the back of the room, and Crimson twisted in her seat. *Surely there wasn't someone else who had fallen for the maire's charms?* But she couldn't make out who it was in the dim light.

"Now, let's get a look at the elf who has taken your maire off the shelf. Stand up, darrling." Sibby pulled Ayla to her feet and she waved shyly. "Isn't she gorgeous? I can see what the maire sees in you, darrling. But what do you see in him?"

More laughter and Ayla blushed. She opened her mouth to say something, but it was too quiet to carry. Sibby widened her eyes and mouth as Ayla spoke, then spoke loud enough so everyone could hear. "Well that explains it. He's got a big…" significant pause "…heart. Lucky girl!"

More laughter as Ayla protested before sinking into her seat. Next to her, the maire roared with laughter. Crimson found herself torn between sympathy for her friend and fun at the maire's expense. Then Sibby was at their table, all six feet of them, seven if you included the hair and heels.

"And who do we have here?"

They gave their names.

"Now, ladies, gentlemen, and those who know better. I happen to know something about one of the people on this table. Miss Crimson Brouderer, will you stand up?"

Roaring filled Crimson's ears. Her legs turned to jelly. She swallowed and forced herself to stand and wave to the room, one hand holding onto the back of her chair for support.

"Now, what we have here, my darrlings, is the best designer in the queendom, and recently appointed guilder."

Crimson let out the breath she had held in as the room clapped. This was fine. She gave a weak smile.

"But, what I found out yesterday is that Crimson Brouderer has never been to one of my shows before." Sibby shook their head in mock sadness. "Can you imagine? She's lived in Saffron Vale for almost two years and has never come to one of my shows. What we have here is a Sibby Show first timer!"

Crimson's knees shook, and her head lightened. Where was Sibby going with this?

"Now, why don't you come to the stage with me, and we'll sort that out? Don't worry," another exaggerated wink to the audience, "I'll be gentle."

Chapter 11

~ Crimson puts on a show ~

CRIMSON'S KNEES LOCKED. HER vision swam, the candlelight blurring into blobs of flame. She couldn't get up on stage with a seasoned performer like Sibby. She clutched the back of the chair while the crowd chanted her name.

"Crimson! Crimson! Crimson!"

Beside her, Lief got to his feet and murmured something to Sibby.

"Well, what do you know, folks? Looks like we've got two new initiates in tonight. Give it up for Lief!" Sibby's voice came from a distance.

"Red." The deep voice was close to her ear. She snapped her head round and met Lief's chocolate gaze. "You can do this.

I'm with you."

He took her hand in his larger one, the warmth of him seeping into her skin and bringing her back into the room.

"I've made a total fool of myself."

He grinned. "Not yet."

Crimson swallowed, but she didn't pull her hand away as he led her in Sibby's wake up onto the stage.

"Now, as there's two of you. I thought we'd have a…Dance Off!"

The crowd exploded at Sibby's words. *What in the queendom was a 'dance off'?* Sibby waved the audience back to a low murmur. "But first, you need to know some moves. We'll start simple with a Saffron Vale classic; the lobster. Arms out, across your chest, up to your head, out to the side, and clack those claws." They demonstrated.

Crimson met Lief's gaze. He shrugged and copied the felinix. Crimson tried her best and found her hands could keep up with Sibby's dance. *Fine. It's fine.* Maybe if she told herself enough times, it would be true.

"Then we've got the duckwalk. Bend your knees. That's it, down to the ground. And strut."

How could they do that in those heels? Crimson almost fell over copying the duckwalk move.

"Grreat job! Now let's get some music and feel free to add your own moves. Gary – let's play one everyone knows." Sibby cued the band, and the strains of a popular song about finding love in Capital City swirled around them.

Crimson closed her eyes and started slow, swaying her hips in time with the music. At a cheer from the crowd, she opened them to see Lief doing the lobster move Sibby had demonstrated. A laugh bubbled from her chest at the sight of the tall woodsman pouting along. She risked a twirl, her skirt flaring out from her body.

"Come on, Crimson, are you going to let him win?" Sibby hissed behind her, grabbing her hands and lifting them into the lobster dance.

"There's no letting me win when I'm the better dancer." Lief shimmied his hips and dropped down into something that might have been the duckwalk. Sibby laughed and released Crimson.

Crimson raised her eyebrows. "That's fighting talk." The crowd melted away, and it was her and Lief in a dance battle. She put two fingers to her eyes, then pointed them at the large man still crouched on the floor.

"Bring it on." He leaned back on his elbows and kicked his legs out. Much more of that and the seams of his trousers would rip.

Crimson lifted her skirts and kicked off her pine-green leather boots. In her stockinged feet, she danced a jig before, carried by the music, she pranced down the steps into the audience and pulled Ayla to her feet. They linked arms and cavorted like they had back in Oasis, chanting the words that had heard performed by buskers and in rare outings to the concert hall. "I met my love in Capital City where drinks ain't cheap but the women are pretty!"

Crimson laughed and released the elf, who coaxed the maire to his feet. "They're playing our song, Jojo."

Maire Bowan needed no more encouragement than a smile and he was up on his hooved feet with a broad grin, hopping and spinning in time with the jaunty beat. His satyr magic swept across the room. Crimson could feel it in the way her movements became more lithe, in how her smile spread and her fear melted away, replaced by a euphoric exuberance that lifted her kicks and gave her the confidence to swoosh her skirts in time with the music. She embraced the maire's infectious joy and spun again and again until the crowd was a blur of faces and streaking candlelight.

The music came to a close with a triumphant finale of strings and horns as the audience stamped their feet and chorused the final words 'and that's how I met my love in Capital City'.

Crimson's chest heaved as she brought her dance to the end. Lief collapsed on the floor and stayed sat down as Sibby raised both their hands aloft.

"Well folks, that was entertaining. And I think I have to declare a draw! I'd have either of you as my back up dancers any day! Give them another round of applause!"

Crimson headed back to her seat. Now the satyr magic had faded, she was keen to hide back in the relative anonymity of the audience. The others congratulated her and then Lief as he followed behind.

A server brought over a jug of scrumpy for the table. "Compliments of Sibby," she said as she plonked the jug down on the wood.

Crimson took a small amount, still scarred from her hangover, then poured for the rest of the table. "You really leaned into the duckwalk," she said as she passed Lief his flagon.

"Want to know a secret, Red?" Lief leaned in and lowered his voice. "I couldn't get back up."

Crimson snorted. "I knew it."

Chapter 12

~ *Confronting the parents* ~

THE FOLLOWING DAY, CRIMSON stretched and added another flourish to her design for Ayla's wedding dress before scratching it out and starting again. Ruffles wouldn't suit her. Ayla loved simplicity. She sighed. This was harder than she'd expected, and her friend was no help at all. Every time she asked Ayla what she wanted, the elf said that she trusted Crimson's judgement.

She yawned. Sibby's show had gone on late into the night, and today Crimson suffered the side effects of a late night and the scrumpy. Even the half mug that she'd drunk had given her a fuzzy head that had lasted well into the afternoon. Although at least she didn't feel like the waking dead. Not like the first time she'd consumed scrumpy and had mistaken it for apple juice, meaning she'd over-imbibed so much that

Lief had had to care for her the day after.

Crimson shook her head to get any thoughts of certain rugged wardens out of her head. Bad enough they had been on stage together, she did not need to relive every nice thing he'd done for her. Wasn't her pounding head punishment enough?

She switched over to what had become her wedding notebook and added 'design invitations' to the growing to do list scrawled there. Crimson rubbed her temples and took a sip of water. Stitches, but there was so much to do and Ayla and the maire seemed to think it would all magically happen in time. Perhaps if she could access the aether…but – she did some rough mental calculations – her letter would take another few days to arrive, then Artor had to draft a reply and post it. If he could even give her guidance on how to access the aether.

The bell above the shop entrance tinkled and Crimson lifted her head from her designs to see a mountain of fabric in every colour of the rainbow enter with two bird feet sticking out from the bottom of the pile.

"Ig, lovely to see you."

The small tylluan mumbled something from behind the stack of material he carried and shuffled to the counter. Crimson raced to help him and together they got the fabric safely on the wooden countertop.

Crimson ran her fingers over the satin. "It's beautiful. How did you get it so white?"

"A combination of bleaching the fabric with sunlight and ultramarine."

"Isn't that blue?" Crimson lifted the first bolt up to the light and squinted at it.

"Yes! That's the thing. A trace of blue brightens the fabric so in most visible spectrums, it appears whiter."

"Really?" It sounded bonkers. But much of what Ig said sounded strange to her.

"It's all to do with the subtractive model of colour perception."

"So everyone sees it as white?"

Ig thought for a moment. "Perhaps not everyone. Werewolves, for example, might see the blue more clearly."

"Then it's a good job there aren't any werewolves coming to the wedding."

Ig furrowed his brow, making his tawny feathers pucker. "A joke? Yes. Ho, ho. Very good. Humour is contextual. I have one for you: why did the tylluan cross the road?"

Crimson opened her mouth to ask why when the bell tinkled again and Pollonius entered, practically pushed by Ovelia.

"Lovely to see you," Crimson said with a strained smile. "I didn't realise you'd be here today." She aimed that comment at Ovelia. She hadn't prepared anything to say to the lovers' parents.

"Nonsense. When Dilly said you were designing all the clothes for the maire's wedding, we had to come and get an order in. Afternoon Ignatius."

Crimson's eyebrows shot up. Would she have to design clothes for everyone attending this wedding? She felt woozy.

"Now, do you need to measure us? I was thinking yellow and white, like the inside of an egg…or perhaps feathers."

"Feathers?"

Pollonius nodded. "I can get some off the chickens."

"Actually, I wanted to talk to–"

The bell rang again and Greezi swept in with Hamlet. "Crimson, I hear you're organising catering for the wedding. What do you think about roast gammon? I can do a marmalade glaze – oh, you're here." The orc sniffed as she noticed Pollonius. "Perhaps we can discuss catering arrangements another time." She turned to leave.

"She's not going to go with your ham for a wedding meal," Pollonius said, folding his arms.

Greezi whipped round and glared down at the dwarf. "What then? You can't think anyone wants stinky eggs at a wedding. Besides, ham is versatile."

"Versatile? You mean you can cut it thick or thin? Hah."

"It's not like you can do anything with eggs."

Pollonius held up a hand and began listing types of eggs on his fingers. "Scrambled, boiled, poached, with mayonnaise, devilled–"

"I, for one, have always wondered what ham and eggs might taste like together," said Ig.

The shop fell silent. Greezi looked like she might explode, and Pollonius' face went an unnatural purplish red that Crimson couldn't name.

Crimson stepped out from behind the counter and stepped between the two parents, holding up her hands in a gesture of peace. "I did want to talk to you about something."

Greezi ground her tusks together, but Pollonius bowed low. "Of course, there is no need to make a scene in Crimson's shop." He turned on a bright smile. "What did you want to talk about? If it's a discount on the catering, then I'm sure we can work something out."

Greezi curled her lips up, exposing her tusks in more of a grimace than a smile but it would do.

"Why don't you take a seat? Through here. Ig, would you mind staying?" Crimson wanted a witness in case things turned sour, which they were almost certain to.

Ovelia placed her hand on Hamlet's back and shoved him towards the door. "This sounds like an important conversation, so we'll just…"

"Stay!" Crimson almost shouted. "You must all stay. Now, come through and I'll make a cup of tea." Tea was neutral. And had the benefit of taking time to brew so everyone could calm down.

"Got any biscuits?" Ig peered into an empty tin and then moved onto the cupboards.

"Try the corner cupboard."

He found a brown paper package and unwrapped it to reveal sugar coated shortbread. Crimson handed him a plate patterned with purple crocuses – crocii? – and stood by the kettle waiting for the familiar whistle that heralded boiling water, hopping from foot to foot and trying out phrases in her head. Was it better to get straight to the point or ease them in? And did they truly not know that their children were madly in love?

By the way the dwarf and the orc stared daggers at each other, Crimson was surprised that the air between them didn't spontaneously combust. Maybe their hatred for each other blinded them to everything else.

After years, or so it seemed, the kettle boiled, and Crimson poured the steaming hot water into a teapot decorated with yet more crocus flowers. Whoever had owned this shop before her had committed to a theme in their crockery.

Once everyone had a mug of tea and a shortbread biscuit, Crimson took a breath. "Now, I did want to talk to you about something important."

"Well? I haven't got all day. The chickens need feeding," Pollonius said around a mouthful of crumbs.

Greezi snorted and rolled her eyes.

Pollonius turned up his glare until the daggers became swords.

"It's about your children," Crimson blurted.

Greezi pulled Hamlet close. "What's wrong, darling? Has

he hurt you?"

Pollonius' brow wrinkled. "Ovelia? What's going on?"

"They're in love." There. She'd said it. Crimson nibbled on her shortbread, unable to enjoy the sugary flavour or melt in the mouth texture.

"So, you know who he's in love with?" Greezi asked. "Good. Out with it. He's been skulking around for months, and I knew it was a girl. Or boy. Who is it?"

"Ovelia," Pollonius clasped her hand in his, "this is marvellous news! Is it serious?"

Hamlet buried his head in his hands.

"They don't understand," wailed Ovelia, tearing at her long hair.

Crimson took a breath. "Your children are in love. With each other."

Chapter 13

~ *The aftermath* ~

"WHAT?!" GREEZI EXPLODED OUT of her seat, sending it flying to the floor.

"Nonsense," said Pollonius. "Tell her it's nonsense, Ovelia."

Ovelia started sobbing and ran out of the shop.

Hamlet stared after her, looked back at his mother, then back at the kitchen door. "See what you've done." He hurried after Ovelia.

"Get back here, Hamlet!" Greezi stamped her foot, causing the cups to clatter on the table.

"Oh my," said Ig, helping himself to another shortbread biscuit.

"Everyone, calm down," said Crimson, jumping to her feet.

"Calm down? Calm down!" Greezi shoved a finger in Crimson's face. "This is your doing, filling their heads with this rubbish. As if my boy could ever love a scrambled egg like her."

"For once, we are in perfect agreement," sniffed Pollonius. "There is no way my darling Ovelia would choose that pig. We are leaving."

"Stop!" Crimson shouted, surprising even herself with the force of her voice.

Greezi and Pollonius stopped in their tracks and faced her, eyes dark with anger.

Crimson swallowed. "You might not like it, but it's true. They love each other and they love you, too. Not being able to be together is killing them. Literally. Do you know what their plan was? They were going to pretend to die. All so they didn't have to tell you about their love. They thought you'd prefer it if they were dead rather than together. It's ridiculous."

Greezi sank to the floor, her face paling to a sage green.

Pollonius swayed where he stood. "What?"

Ig stood and offered him a biscuit. "Sugar and tea help with shock," he said, sounding as if he were reading from a textbook.

"Tea! Yes, let's make another cup of tea and we can talk. Why don't you sit down, Pollonius?" Crimson busied herself with brewing more tea while both Greezi and Pollonius stared at fixed points on her buttercup yellow kitchen walls.

As she placed a cup in front of Greezi, the orc snapped out of whatever trance she was in. "This is your fault."

"My fault? Your son's the one who prances around the town in those tight clothes. Villy didn't stand a chance."

"Your daughter must have led him on. My Hamlet would never look at her unless she made the first move."

"Blaming them isn't helping," said Crimson, plonking her mug on the table with such force that some of it spilled onto the wooden surface in a dark puddle. "As far as I understand it, they're both madly in love with each other."

Greezi folded her arms and went back to staring at the wall.

"I don't understand why this is such a problem. Love should be celebrated."

Pollonius sighed and pulled at his beard. "It's complicated."

"It's not complicated at all. That old witch Eggy Henning tricked my Great Grandad out of his life savings–"

"Rubbish! Tricky Hamble tricked her out of her chicken farm. It's taken generations to rebuild our birds to the champion stock they were through careful breeding."

Crimson banged her hand on the table. "You are fighting about something that happened generations ago! You need to let it go, or you're going to lose your children."

"You wouldn't understand. You're an outsider." Greezi shook her head, causing the gold bands around her tusks to catch the light.

Crimson narrowed her eyes. She had been here for over a year, and she felt more at home here than in all her years living as an apprentice in Oasis. "I may not be a Saffron Vale native, but I know enough to tell when people are being stupid. And your stupidity is going to cost you Hamlet and Ovelia."

"Well, I never." Pollonius got to his feet and stalked out.

Greezi followed, still shaking her head. "A Hamble will never be with a Henning, and that's final."

Crimson trembled as she watched them go before she collapsed into her chair and laid her head on the table.

"I thought that went well," said Ig, spraying crumbs across the room.

Crimson gave a weak laugh. "If that was well, I'd hate to see what bad looked like."

"They could have started throwing things."

Crimson's laugh grew until her entire body shook and she lifted her head. "Good one, Ig."

The tylluan gave her a confused smile. "Was it? I'll write that down." He pulled a small, leatherbound notebook from his pocket and scribbled something down before tucking it away. "Well, ta ta for now." He straightened his jacket and smoothed down his feathers. "I've got to pick something up from the forge."

Crimson raised her eyebrows. "Are you finally going to tell Milus how you feel?"

Ig choked on air. "What?" He flattened his feathers again.

"You should, you know. Tell him, I mean."

Ig pulled out his notebook again and ran a finger down a well-worn page. "No, no, no. That's the final stage. I am on step three of my plan to become better acquaintances; saying hello when we see each other. And I've ordered something from him, which will allow us to exchange pleasantries, moving us to step four."

"I thought that was where you were last year."

"No – look – step one was acknowledging each other with a dip of the head. Step three is verbal greetings."

"And what's stage five?"

Ig gave a small, nervous hoot. "Well…that's the steps to become an acquaintance, then I have a new list for becoming friends. For example, we could discuss more meaningful topics and eventually, I could ask him if he'd like to attend a social gathering where I will also be. But it's far too soon for that."

"How long have you known him?"

"Only six years. Barely any time at all."

"If you think you like him, you should tell him. Love shouldn't be a secret. Look what keeping their feelings hidden from their parents has done to Hamlet and Ovelia."

Ig smoothed the front of his waistcoat down. "Perhaps. I shall study it some more. There must be a formula for emotions." He jotted something down in his book. "So, when are you and Lief going to 'get together', as they say?"

It was Crimson's turn to splutter. "What do you mean?"

"You like him. He likes you." Ig frowned. "If it's obvious to me, then it must be obvious to you. Did you not say that you should tell someone if you like them? And you've attended a social gathering together and," Ig consulted his list, "eaten alone together. What's left?"

"Lief doesn't like me."

Ig's feathered eyebrows knotted together. "No? Then my observations are entirely incorrect. How fascinating."

"Are you studying me?"

"I observe everyone. Now, I must dash if I want to pick up the tools before Milus shuts up shop." Ig left her then and Crimson collapsed back onto the table, the weight of designing the perfect dress for both Ayla and Sibby and sorting out the mess that was Greezi and Pollonius pressing down on her.

If only she could disappear into the tegs' realm to get away from this mess. Crimson closed her eyes and passed her hands in front of her in a way that she thought was magical. Nothing happened. No surprises there. She'd have to sort this mess out without magical assistance.

Chapter 14

~ An idea ~

A WALK. THAT WOULD clear her head. "Come on, Smudge."

She led the small dragon out of the shop and onto the High Street. But where now? Crimson turned her head towards town. Too crowded. She could head down to Ig's lighthouse, and the beach beyond. Maybe the Great Lobster would be there with some words of wisdom for her. Although what advice they could give her on dress design or getting stubborn parents to listen to their children, she didn't know.

The forest it was, then. She set off on the path out of town with Smudge sniffing at every weed and interesting looking corner on the way before laying down his own scents.

Crimson followed the path to the edge of the forest before veering off to the side and walking through the meadow that skirted the trees. She was a coward. The trodden path led to Lief's cottage, and she couldn't go back there. Not when he was making a home with *her*. She could see them now; settling down for an evening meal – venison probably, with greens – Bircha cooking with the flair of a gourmet chef while smiling at Lief setting the table – and then they'd snuggle up by the fire under one of the cosy blankets.

Crimson kicked her foot at a dandelion, sending seeds flying through the air. She rubbed her temples. It was no good. She couldn't allow Lief's choices to affect her so. She didn't even care for him, so what did it matter? If she told herself that enough times, she might believe the lie.

Crimson collapsed onto the grass and got out her design book. She needed to focus on Ayla's wedding dress and Sibby's commission. As if sensing her distress, Smudge gambolled over and rubbed his head against her knees. Crimson scratched behind his ear and told him not to worry about her and to enjoy himself. With a flick of his tail, he ran back into the long grass, a flash of purple between the long stems.

Crimson closed her eyes and took three cleansing breaths. The sounds of the meadow surrounded her; the swish of the unmown grass like the sound of silk brushing against a table, the birdsong, sweet and unhurried, and high above her, a red kite kee-yahed as it swirled through the sky.

When Crimson opened her eyes, she still didn't have inspiration, but she was calm enough to start drawing. That was the beauty of a rural vale like Saffron Vale; it was slower than a city or the large town where she grew up. While she sometimes missed the bustle of Oasis, here she had time to stop and think and places where she could be alone without a crowd of people passing by.

Crimson sketched a meadow flower and tried turning the form of the petals into a neckline. She scrunched up her nose. That didn't work, but maybe another flower would. Fixing on nature as a muse, Crimson drew stems and leaves and blades of grass, but nothing quite said Ayla to her.

Smudge laid a dandelion head at Crimson's feet and stared at her until she'd congratulated him on his prize before he ran off to chase a grasshopper that chirruped in the long grass.

She picked up the dandelion clock and twirled it in her fingers, watching the pale seeds float away without a care in the world. *Lucky seeds.* More bobbed in front of her, caught in the swirling currents of air as if they danced to a beat that no one else could hear.

Much like Sibby.

Crimson tilted her head and studied the seeds more closely. Inspiration flooded her. Suddenly, she wasn't grasping at loose threads for ideas, and they flowed fully formed into her mind in hot flashes that widened her eyes and caught her breath.

She pulled her design book out of her satchel and began sketching with a fervour she hadn't experienced in a long time.

Crimson could picture the dress in its entirety – the flowing skirt, the tight bodice, the way the seams joined in perfect harmony with the material. But what fabric?

She plucked a seed from those remaining on the dandelion clock. Something wispy and insubstantial but with structure. Maybe lace? Or starched netting? She scribbled that down. It was a specialist material, and she'd have to place an order with ATOZ, the most widespread trading company in the queendom. If they couldn't help her, then nobody could.

And if Sibby wore white, then Ayla should shine in sunflower yellow – a nod to her favourite flower and the saffron harvested in the vale. Yes!

Crimson sat there until the sun set and it was too dark to see the paper in her book, which was now covered with sketches and notes. With a satisfied sigh, she pushed herself to her feet and stood, stretching out her cramped shoulders.

"Come on, Smudge. Let's go home."

The small dragon snorted his agreement and lifted his head out from a rabbit hole. He sneezed, dislodging the dirt around his snout, and setting a patch of dry grass on fire.

Crimson stamped it out, lifting her skirts high so they didn't catch. Once she was satisfied that there was no danger of a stray spark growing into a wildfire, she called Smudge again. But the little dragon was nowhere to be seen.

"Smudge. Smudge!" Crimson turned on the spot, squinting in the growing darkness, hoping for a flash of purple scales.

A snuffling came from the trees and Crimson's shoulders

fell. He had disappeared into the forest.

Chapter 15

~ A wolf in Saffron Vale ~

CRIMSON PAUSED AT THE edge of the unkempt trees and looked longingly towards the path that led back to town and civilisation, before clutching her satchel and stepping into the forest. She wouldn't abandon her oldest friend in Saffron Vale to the wilds of the woods.

"Smudge!" She whisper-shouted, hoping that he would come to her.

Crimson's dress snagged on a branch as she crept into the woods, trying her best not to make a noise. These weren't the manicured trees of The Thicket back in Oasis, which was home to sprites and other small folk. These were old, wild trees that looked like they might up and move as soon as your back was turned and then laugh at the joke.

A rustling sound from her left made Crimson snap her head round. She breathed a sigh of relief when she saw it was only a squirrel hopping from branch to branch. Probably trying to get to the safety of his home. Much like she should be doing.

She called for her dragon again, her voice unnatural in this untamed forest. A snap of a twig and Crimson froze. Squirrels weren't the only animals in the woods. On her very first day in Saffron Vale, she had encountered a rogue unicorn intent on mowing her down. Maybe it was still here. And it remembered her scent, marking her as an outsider in its territory.

Crimson backed up until she hit the scratchy bark of an oak tree. Or was it a beech? Who knew? The woods weren't her domain. She was comfortable in the town, where she knew how to get food and could brew a cup of tea whenever she wanted one, not out here where you had to know what was what to avoid getting poisoned.

Now Lief, he would know exactly what to do. He could probably track a dragon even in the dark. A smile curved her lips as she thought about what he would say if he could see her now, how that stupid nickname he had for her would drop from his lips like a private caress as he led her to safety.

What are you doing here, Red?

Her smile disappeared. She shouldn't even be thinking of him. He had chosen someone else. The visit to his house had made that clear. He probably had a pet name for Bircha, too. Brown, maybe, to match her hair. That was unkind. Bircha's hair was more chestnut, anyway. Maybe that was his name for her; Chestnut.

A squeal of pain jerked her from her spiralling thoughts about her love life, or lack thereof. "Smudge!"

Crimson ran towards the sound, ignoring the fear that thudded through her veins and the tearing fabric as her dress caught on spiky brambles that reached into her path. Her dragon was in trouble!

She tripped over a trailing root and tumbled into a clearing. The grass glistened silver under the light of the full moon. Crimson lifted her head, spitting out leaves.

An enormous wolf stood panting on the other side of the clearing. A familiar chirrup drew Crimson's gaze down to where Smudge lay at its feet.

Crimson's heart leapt to her throat. Her fingers dug into the ground and closed around a large stick. She struggled to her feet, batting off trailing clumps of nature that hung on her dress. Crimson held the stick like a bat and planted her feet.

"Now, Mr Wolf, that is my dragon, and I would very much appreciate it if you could leave him alone." The wolf tilted its head to one side. Crimson made a small swiping motion with the stick. She didn't like violence, but for the sake of her dragon, she'd fight. "I don't want to have to use this."

A snort came from the wolf's mouth, as if it laughed at her.

Smudge raced over to her and jumped up into her arms. Crimson dropped her stick and hugged him close, squeezing his warm body against hers. "Thank the Artisan you're alright. Now let's go home."

Smudge licked her face, leaving dragon slobber on her cheek before squirming free and darting back to the wolf, nuzzling against one enormous paw.

"What are you doing?" Crimson hissed. "Get back here. We have to go. It could eat you."

The wolf snorted again and lay down, pushing against her small dragon with its huge wet nose.

Crimson clenched her fists. *Stupid dragon*. He was going to get them both killed. Maybe she should just go and come back in the morning. Even as she thought the words, she knew it was rubbish. There was no way she'd leave her friend in the forest, even if he was a stupid dragon.

Another wolf trotted out of the trees and sniffed the air. It was smaller than the first one but with similar colouring. Perhaps they were related. Or maybe all wolves looked the same. Crimson didn't know. Her entire experience with wolves came from one bizarre encounter in the Capital. Now she thought about it, the larger wolf looked similar to the city wolf…something about the facial expression and the way the ears flicked.

The new wolf came up to Crimson and pushed its face into her hands. She scratched behind its ears, not knowing what else to do.

The first wolf let out a warning growl. Crimson froze. It prowled over and shoulder-barged the smaller wolf out of the way.

The second wolf snarled and leapt at the first one, snapping its teeth. Crimson held still. She didn't even breathe, hoping to avoid the attention of the growling mass of wolf flesh that fought in front of her.

The wolves broke apart and circled each other. The smaller one pounced, fast as quicksilver. But the larger one sidestepped and snapped its jaws around the second wolf's throat. The smaller wolf let out a whine and the first wolf growled before releasing it.

The second wolf snarled, and the bigger wolf bared its teeth and maintained eye contact until the new wolf looked away for a split second, then rolled over to expose its belly.

The first wolf sat on its haunches and the second got to its feet, walked right up to the large wolf and licked its face. The wolf let out a huff so similar to a human sigh that Crimson had to laugh.

She covered her mouth with her hands as both wolves' heads snapped round to her. *Idiot.* Their playfighting forgotten, now they had one target: her.

Crimson backed away. Her heart thundered in her chest. Could wolves hear heartbeats? One more thing she didn't know about wolves. If she got out of this alive, she'd have to see if she could find a book about lupine behaviour. Crimson shook her head to stop the stupid thoughts. She was about to die and she was thinking about learning more about the creatures ready to rip her to shreds. She had bigger things to worry about.

"Don't kill me."

The wolves stayed still, two sets of amber eyes staring at her.

"I have to make my best friend a wedding dress. I can't let her down."

The larger wolf nosed the smaller one, as if to say 'get out of here, you're scaring her'. Great. Now she imagined that she could understand these wild beasts.

The smaller wolf seemed to grin. It chuffed and wagged its tail before heading back into the forest for whatever wolfy business it had.

"Thank you." Crimson didn't know what else to say to the enormous wolf who remained, so she babbled on, "Ayla will be ever so grateful if you let us go. And so will the maire. He'll probably name one of his curvy carts after you."

The wolf shook its head.

"I know. I think they're bonkers too."

The wolf moved closer, treading slowly on the trampled grass, as if it didn't want to scare her away. Crimson almost laughed again. She was terrified, and she didn't think her feet would move even if she wanted them to.

The wolf sat down in front of her, not taking its gaze from her face. Crimson bit her lip.

"I know you," Crimson whispered. "You're the wolf from

the Capital." What was she saying? That was impossible. The Capital was miles away. There was no way that a wolf could travel that distance, was there? And even if it did, how could this wolf be the same one who had rescued her from attackers in the Capital City?

The wolf cocked its head to one side and its tongue lolled out of its mouth, as if it grinned at her.

And, deep in her heart, Crimson knew that it was the same animal. It was the same sensation as when she'd decided to come to Saffron Vale and abandon her unfulfilling life in Oasis. She had known that was right, and she knew, in the place somewhere between her heart and her stomach, that she was right about the wolf too.

"Who are you?"

The wolf sighed and lay down in front of her, looking up with puppy dog eyes. It looked so sad and abandoned that Crimson's heart swelled and she reached out without thinking, stroking the wolf's thick fur, relishing the softness. She sank to the ground next to this creature that she couldn't understand and wrapped her arms around its neck. It leaned into her, and something slid into place in her soul. Crimson felt like she was meant to be here, with this wolf.

Which was the sort of thought a crazy person would have. Maybe she was mad. That would explain why she was hugging a wild creature. Crimson let go with a little cough.

The wolf grunted and shoved its face back into Crimson's

hands, making her give a shaky laugh. "Well, you know what you want."

It snorted at that.

"So, you're not going to eat us then, Mr Wolf?"

The wolf lifted its head and blew a hot breath into her face, making her grimace.

"Then, may we go?" Crimson whispered, running her hand through the velvet fur behind its ear.

The wolf sighed but got to its feet and took two steps towards town.

"You're going to come back to town with us?" The night couldn't get much weirder and the wolf had the chance to eat them already, so Crimson scrambled up. "Come on, Smudge."

She picked up the small dragon, who yawned loudly and clambered up to her shoulders, where he looped his body around her neck like a scarf and closed his eyes, settling against her skin and lending her his warmth.

The wolf stayed by her side, close enough for its fur to brush against her swishing skirts as they ambled back to town. Crimson wanted to prolong her time with this majestic animal, enjoying its silent, supportive company, grateful for the way it nudged her so she avoided the roots that jutted from the ground.

Back on the path, it accompanied her to the edge of town. Crimson walked a further three paces before she realised the wolf had stopped and now sat in the middle of the path, its amber eyes tracking her every move.

"You won't go any further with me, Mr Wolf?"

The wolf looked at the ground, then back up at her before getting reluctantly to its feet. Crimson's heart swelled knowing that this animal would stay by her side, but then her stomach sank. She couldn't ask it to do that, to go into a place that wasn't its natural habitat just so she could get some comfort.

Crimson knelt in the path, so her face was level with the wolf's. "I won't ask you to do something you're not comfortable with, Mr Wolf. Thank you for accompanying me so far." She caressed his ears, imprinting that soft velvet texture against her fingertips before leaving him on the path.

Chapter 16

~ *Bircha confronts Crimson* ~

HEN CRIMSON WENT TO open up her shop the next morning, she saw Bircha leaning against the doorframe, arms folded and face pinched in a frown.

Crimson swallowed and hesitated a moment before she crossed the room and unlocked the door.

Bircha barged in, sending the bell above the door jangling. The tall woman winced and glared at the small bell.

Crimson took a step back from the hulking chestnut-haired woman towering over her. "Can I help you with something? The hosiery is my most popular item, or there's off the shelf dresses ready." She took a moment to look Bircha up and down. "I think I have your size."

"What are you doing?"

"Opening the shop."

Bircha crossed her arms over her chest. "With Lief."

"That is rich coming from you."

The tall woman's brow furrowed. "What's that supposed to mean?"

"Never mind," Crimson muttered, turning her back on Bircha to open the shutters to let in the morning light. Still ignoring the fuming woman behind her, Crimson began fussing with the stock in the window, tweaking a bolt of sapphire blue material here and adjusting the mannequin with her signature pocket dress there.

"So you don't care about him at all?"

Crimson whirled round. "I want him to be happy. Clearly that doesn't include me." She threw up her hands. "Why am I even talking to you about this?"

"I want to talk. Lief's miserable and I know it's because of you."

Crimson retreated behind her counter, wanting a barrier between her and Bircha. She traced her fingers along the measuring stick that Lief had cut into the wooden countertop – back when they had worked together to fix up the dilapidated shop.

Undeterred, Bircha placed her elbows on the counter and leaned forward. "I want him to be happy. Why don't you want to be with him? He's great. A bit of a grump sometimes, sure, but he's got a good heart."

"I know that." Crimson didn't need anyone to list out Lief's good qualities. She spent enough time alone at night thinking about all of them, and then listing all the reasons she should forget him. Number one being the woman crowding her in her own shop.

"So, what's the matter?" Bircha pressed on, studying Crimson with her cinnamon-coloured eyes.

Crimson frowned. Was this a trick question? "You're with him."

Bircha rolled her eyes. "Only for a little while. I'll head back to the Capital soon and then he'll be all alone."

Crimson bit her lip. "You're not staying?" She shook her head. It didn't matter. He had chosen Bircha over her back in Innton, after their kiss. And he'd lived with her for months in his cabin. Just because he was fine with an open relationship didn't mean that she was and what if Bircha came back into their lives? Would he choose her again?

Oblivious to Crimson's swirling thoughts, Bircha sniffed. "No. I've had enough of Saffron Vale. I get itchy if I'm here for too long. Too many bad memories after Mum and Dad died." She lifted her hand as Crimson started to offer an apology for their deaths. "It happened a long time ago, but Lief stayed on. He's got a strong sense of loyalty, and he felt he had to protect the forest, live their legacy. As if they care now they're running with the twin moons up there."

Bircha shivered. "No, I had to get out of here. I haven't been back for," she scratched the back of her neck as she thought, "oh, about ten years. I've got my life in the Capital, and I get to travel the queendom and beyond. I was just finishing up in Turtle Bay when I got word that my brother had tried to see me in the Capital, so I hurried over to Innton, caught up with him and promised to spend some time here. I might even stay for the wedding."

Crimson's mind raced trying to keep up with all the information. "You're not in a relationship with Lief." She had to say it out loud to make sure she hadn't misunderstood.

"With my brother? That's disgusting."

"Your brother? Lief is your brother." Crimson paused over each word. So much made sense now. The similar eyes and face shapes, even the similar builds; both muscular and outdoorsy in a way Crimson would never be. That was why she had moved in with him as soon as they'd got to Saffron Vale; naturally he'd offer his sister a bed.

And, of course, he would want to meet her for breakfast at Innton, especially if he hadn't seen her for a decade. And that explained why his face softened when he looked at her or spoke about her. Family was sacred. Crimson remembered her own mother with a deep fondness and knew she would do anything to spend time with her if she could.

Bircha gave her a look that asked how stupid she could be. "Yes." Her eyes narrowed. "Why? Did you think we were…? With him?" She made a retching sound.

"Are you alright?" Now that Crimson knew they weren't rivals, she could be compassionate.

Bircha dry heaved again. "Give me a minute. I can't even…with Lief?"

"I'll get you some water." Crimson rushed to the kitchen that backed onto the shop and pumped some water, giving herself time to think. All of her unhappiness was self-inflicted. Lief had never been in a relationship with Bircha. She flushed. Stitches, she had treated him like a piece of mud on her shoe, punished him for something he hadn't done. Why hadn't she swallowed her pride and talked to him? This could have been cleared up months ago.

Her hand pumped up and down with ferocious speed as she berated herself. He wasn't Namu. He wouldn't betray her friendship – her love – and throw her away for selfish gain. All he'd ever done was help her, and see her for who she was, and he hadn't backed away from her challenges.

Cold water splashed over her hand as the cup ran over making her jump. Crimson stopped pumping and grabbed a cloth. Once the cup was dry and filled with an appropriate amount of water, she took it back to the shop and handed it to Bircha, who drained it and wiped her lips with the back of her hand.

"Do you, do you think he'd forgive me for how I've acted?" Crimson's voice was small, and she couldn't meet Bircha's eyes.

Lief's sister sighed. "That's the thing about my stupid big

brother; he's always ready to think the best of people. Even me." Her throaty voice gentled. "Why don't we find out?"

Crimson swallowed and nodded.

"Leave everything to me." With that, Bircha left, leaving Crimson feeling small and alone in her shop.

Chapter 17

~ Games Night ~

CRIMSON PLACED A CARD down and met Lief's gaze, attempting to send him a psychic message about the cards she had left in her hand. It was her first time playing Chase the Queen with a deck of cards similar to the standard deck Crimson had seen before when she'd played the popular Bread and Butter card game.

It included the same suits of Jam, Jelly, Bread and Butter, but that's where the similarities ended because this deck included Kings, Queens and Knights. The game was both simple and fiendishly complex with people playing cards while trying to keep the Queens in hand with bonus points, depending on which Queen you had at the end of the game[2]. And Bircha had tried to explain something about the Wandering Jester card, which allowed you to swap random cards in players' hands, but Crimson hadn't fully understood and held onto her Jester.

The game was played in teams of two, as every game so far this evening had been. Bircha had insisted on pairing up Lief and Crimson every time and so they had mimed their way through Guess the Word and had a very strange game of Create a Story where Bircha had managed to turn every tale into a romance. Subtle.

Lief frowned and played the nine of Butter. Crimson groaned then straightened her face.

"You're too easy to read, my girl," said the maire with a laugh and he played his ten, sitting back in his chair and grinning from ear to ear.

Lief raised his eyebrows at Crimson. She took a deep breath and yelled, "Jester," before Ayla could play her card.

Ayla held out her remaining cards. The middle one was ever so slightly higher than the rest, tempting Crimson to pick it. But she knew her friend well and chose the left-hand one. She grinned as she turned it over and saw the Queen of Butter smiling back at her. Ayla's face dropped as Crimson replaced it with the three of Jam from her hand and the elf had to pass.

---

[2] Naturally the Queen of Bread beat the Queens of Butter, Jelly and Jam.

But she'd miscounted the Jesters left and Bircha stole the Queen from Crimson, meaning that Crimson and Lief lost the trick and the game.

Crimson got up as Hardy insisted on counting up the scores again. "Does anyone need anything?" she offered as she headed to the kitchen space in Lief's cottage for a refill on her drink, and maybe one of Ayla's iced biscuits.

There had been a bit of tension when both Ayla and Dilly had turned up with plates of sweet treats, but Bircha had brushed over it and, after a shoulder nudge from Duncan, Dilly had been on her best behaviour with Ayla. She had even offered to make her tea when the elf visited her café. But there was a wicked tilt to Dilly's smile when she said that, and Crimson had made a mental note to warn Ayla about taking tea from Dilly without knowing what it was called. Her embarrassing experience with the Lovers' Delight tea still loomed large in her mind.

Crimson refilled her earthenware mug with cloudy lemonade and considered the iced biscuits. Ayla had outdone herself with delicate icing flowers picked out in garden scenes. Almost too beautiful to eat. Almost. Crimson selected one with tiny crocuses – crocii? – and took a bite.

"Good choice, Red."

"Mmfh," Crimson said through a mouthful of biscuit, startled at Lief's silent approach before a crumb hit the back of her throat, causing a coughing fit. How could someone so large move so quietly? She covered her mouth with her hand

and tried to stop the coughs, which only made them worse.

"Are you alright?"

Crimson waved him off, still bent over, choking on the biscuit. He slapped her on the back. Crimson swallowed and managed to gasp down a breath.

"Do you always sneak up on people?" Unsure what to say, Crimson reverted to lashing out. Stitches, why did she always have to push Lief away? It was as if her mouth wanted to sabotage her heart.

"You're very red."

"It's warm in here."

"Shall we go outside?"

Crimson swallowed. A large part of her screamed that was a bad idea, but another, sappier part said that she should. She decided to listen to her heart, and nodded, glad to leave the crowded cottage for a moment.

At the table, Bircha and Dilly argued with Ig and Duncan about whether to start a game of Daggers.

"But what'll we bet?" asked Bircha, shuffling the cards between her long fingers.

"How about Strip Daggers?" The maire's eyes gleamed. Ayla giggled.

Crimson hurried out of the door and leaned against the cool wooden wall, closing her eyes for a moment.

"You don't fancy Strip Daggers, then?"

Crimson snorted and looked at Lief. His mouth twisted up at the corner in a mischievous half grin that sent something in her stomach fluttering.

"It's hardly fair," she said, "I'm wearing less clothes than everyone else, apart from Ayla." They were the only two in dresses and the others had trousers, braies, shirts and jackets. And, in the maire's case, an extravagant waistcoat and a hat.

"So you think you'll lose? Good to know."

"I couldn't even understand the rules for Chase the Queen and I've never played Daggers before. I'm not stupid." The dwarfish game card game was fiendishly complex, and all she really knew about it was that it had a reputation for ending in fights in unsavoury taverns.

"No, you're not."

"Was that a compliment?" Crimson teased.

"What if it was?" He moved closer.

Crimson licked her lips. It was so easy to get sucked into his dark gaze and lose herself. But there was something she had to say first. She looked away, down at the ground. "I'm sorry."

"I didn't expect to hear you say that."

Crimson twisted her foot into the dirt. "Am I that horrible?" she whispered. "That you think I can't apologise."

"No!" He lifted her chin up with his forefinger. "I don't think that. I just didn't expect it. And you don't need to apologise."

"I do! Did Bircha tell you…?"

"That you thought we were together? Yes." His lips twitched. "If I'd known why you stopped talking to me for months, I would have explained."

"I know. I'm sorry I jumped to conclusions. I guess I need to learn to trust more."

"You can trust me." His dark eyes were sincere, and Crimson found that she believed him.

"I'm sorry."

"Stop apologising."

"Are you two coming inside?" Dilly appeared as a silhouette at the doorway, arms crossed.

"That depends," Lief said, his gaze still on Crimson, "are we playing Strip Daggers?"

"No! Standard Daggers. Hurry up." Dilly disappeared back inside.

"So, are we alright?" Crimson asked, holding her breath as she waited for the answer.

"We're good, Red. So," Lief shifted his feet, "can I come and see you sometime?"

She smiled up at him. "Yes. But not this week. I'm too busy with wedding things."

Lief groaned. "You don't like making things easy, do you?"

"Hurry up!" Bircha's voice came from inside.

Chapter 18

~ *The maire chooses a best man* ~

LIEF LAID DOWN HIS hand and scooped up his winnings with a grin. They had decided to play with the remains of the biscuits and cakes in place of money – or clothes – and the pile in front of Lief was almost as large as the one in front of Crimson, who had experienced a streak of beginner's luck.

Although both their winnings were dwarfed by Ig's pile of pastries. He hooted about probability of cards any time someone questioned him on his tactics.

"Never mind, Jojo." Ayla yawned. "It's getting late."

"With gamesmanship like that, you should be my best man!" Maire Bowan said, rubbing a hand through his curly hair.

"I thought Hardy was your best man?" Lief asked.

"That wet blanket?" The maire snorted. "No offense." Hardy sniffed and crunched on a biscuit. "He's the officiant." The maire got to his cloven feet and stretched his hand out as he proclaimed. "Lief, warden of this fair vale, will you do me the great honour of being my best man?"

Lief looked around, possibly searching for help, before he sighed. "Yes."

The maire's stubby tail wagged. "Excellent. We shall have to talk about the lobster do. But, for now, my Ayay is tired, and we should away for the night is late and I have my morning tussle with The Golden Acorn crossword puzzle to prepare for."

"We should go too." Dilly nodded to her brother.

"I'll walk you home." Bircha stood, slamming her chair into the wall with a thud.

"Sure." Dilly shrugged while Crimson eyed Bircha with interest. Which petalborn was Lief's sister interested in? Dilly or her strong and silent brother? Dilly grabbed a cake from Ig's pile. "Want to walk back with us, Ig?"

The tylluan hooted his agreement and the three of them shrugged on their coats and headed out the door with Bircha in tow. Ayla and the maire followed behind. Ayla tried to speak to Duncan about his cupcake recipe, but Dilly shut her down.

"I should go too. If I don't let Smudge out, he might decide to pee on my new fabric." It had happened before.

"I'll walk you back."

"I'm sure I can follow the path to town. I found my own way here, after all."

Lief's gaze shot to the forest. "It's not the path to town I'm worried about. There are things in the forest that can be dangerous."

"*You* go in there every day."

He shrugged. "That's my job. Besides, I'm scarier than anything hiding in the trees."

Crimson laughed at that, but Lief remained serious. She twisted her dress in her hands, unsure what to say except, "Come on then."

"You could always stay, you know. If you wanted."

Crimson swallowed, her throat suddenly dry. Was that what she wanted? She shook her head. "What about Bircha?"

"If I know my little sister, she'll be staying over with Dilly tonight."

That answered the question about who she was interested in. Crimson bit her lip. "I have an early start tomorrow."

Lief nodded and put on a smile. "Let's get you home."

Chapter 19

~ Crimson makes a start on the dress ~

THE FOLLOWING DAY WAS normally Crimson's rest day. The one day in the week where she didn't open the shop and she could choose to spend it how she wanted. Sometimes she went for a walk to get inspiration from the vale, sometimes – most often when it rained – she sat reading a book curled up in her bed, listening to the raindrops pelt her window. But today was a day for designing.

She took out her design book and studied her sketches, inspired by the dandelion bloom and the natural colours found in the vale. Crimson transferred the drawings into pattern pieces on the roll of tracing paper she kept under her bed, her charcoal pencil flowing over the paper like water. Normally, she would trust her judgement and forego the patterns, but not when the stakes were so high.

A wedding dress was the central piece of the ceremony. It drew the eyes of every guest to a focal point as the wearer swished up the aisle. It was the most important item of clothing that person would wear in their life – perhaps with the exception of a queen's coronation gown – and people would talk about it for moons after; either with reverence or with sniggers if it went wrong.

But, the primary purpose of wedding attire was to make the client feel like royalty for a day, to make sure they were the centre of attention and capture their style mixed with a little fantasy to elevate them to the best version of themselves. It had to be comfortable, yet extravagant, weighty enough to hang perfectly over the wearer's form, yet light enough that they could wear all day. It was the pinnacle of any dressmaker's creations.

And this was extra special because Crimson was making it for her best friend. It had to be perfect. So she measured everything again, marking any corrections with dark lines before daring to cut out the pieces – not with her fabric scissors! – adding a half inch seam allowance, before pinning them together over a mannequin to check the fit.

It took the entire morning to do that for both Ayla's wedding gown and Sibby's performance dress and took up almost all of her tracing paper. Crimson wiped away the sweat from her forehead as she surveyed her creations.

She stood back, looking them up and down with a critical eye. Any mistakes at this stage would carry over to the gowns themselves, so she had to get this right. Her stomach growled in protest but Crimson ignored it as she adjusted her pins and made sure both gowns were perfect.

Smudge whined at the stairway, and Crimson tucked a final pin in and stepped back for one last look before she let him out. They were good, if she did say so herself. Better than good. These would be her best work, if she could sew them in time.

Her fingers itched to get to work, but another whine from Smudge told her he couldn't wait much longer to get outside so she left the paper there and let him out in the tiny courtyard garden that backed onto the kitchen. It didn't have much; a few neglected pots that sat on the paved earth and a small privy that backed onto the wall, but Crimson took joy in the wildflowers that flourished there without needing any careful tending. Others might call them weeds, but Crimson loved the stubborn determination of the colourful plants that fought to grow in a patch that might normally reject them.

Thinking back, she had always admired the flowers that managed to thrive in the barest of conditions; the dandelions that forced their way between the cracks in pavements, the low creeping vines that insisted on giving walls a splash of vibrant green. Seeing plants that no one wanted revel in being what they were and not just surviving, but thriving against the odds, gave her the strength to keep going whenever she felt like an outsider.

Crimson rolled her shoulders, stretching out muscles that

were taut from hours cutting and pinning, bent over on the floor. Her stomach made itself known again and she wandered back into the kitchen to see what she had in the cupboards. She didn't hold out much hope, given that she couldn't remember the last time she went to the grocers, but maybe there was something.

As expected, her cupboards were almost bare. The only item that was plentiful were the combination of charcoal lumps and fish protein biscuits she had for Smudge. It would have been embarrassing if there were guests, but as it was just her, Crimson made do with a couple of crackers spread with creamy golden butter. The dairy from Saffron Vale was the richest Crimson had ever tasted. She closed her eyes in pleasure, savouring the smooth taste of the salted butter that took the edge off the dry crackers.

To finish her meal, Crimson cut an apple into quarters and ate them slowly. The slower she ate, the more her stomach thought it received and the less it would argue with her later. That was the theory anyway.

She didn't have time for food shopping, or lunch breaks if she wanted to get the pattern pieces cut out of fabric today. Maybe there would even be time to tack the dresses together before sunset. Crimson shook her head, knowing that was too ambitious, but she could dream and the more she got done today, the less she'd have to do tomorrow, and the day after and the day after.

She groaned. Too much to do in too little time. But the best way to make progress was one stitch at a time, so she stretched out her arms one last time, poured a bowl of dragonfood for Smudge and headed back upstairs to her workroom, leaving the back door open so Smudge could come and go as he pleased.

Satisfied with the pattern pieces, Crimson moved to the next stage and unrolled the first fabric she wanted; saffron sunshine. It shimmered in the afternoon light and filled the room with the joy that she always got from the bright yellow colour. She would use this for Ayla's dress – it fit with the saffron theme perfectly – paired with a pale green in the same material as a nod to Ayla's love of nature. And then there would be gemstone embellishments and perhaps splashes of purple to bring in the vale flower; the crocus. Or maybe that would be better as a headpiece. Crimson loved clashing colours in unusual ways, but perhaps a wedding dress wasn't the best place to experiment.

Crimson cut the bodice pieces – all sixteen of them; eight for the corselet to provide support, eight to cover the structural piece. A final eight panels of a lighter material would come later, to allow the saffron sunshine to shine through, along with the gemstones and perhaps some delicate embroidery. A small smile crept onto her face as the creation bloomed in her mind's eye. But first, she had to tack it together.

Crimson reached for her mother's sewing box. It was a plain affair, a simple workwoman's box, but it contained everything she needed for dressmaking. Her slim hands trailed over her assortment of threads, ordered by colour. Her fingers paused on the spool of shimmering emerald green thread that had belonged to her mother. Everything else in the box she had replaced without a second thought as it wore out; needles, pins, other threads. But she couldn't bring herself to use her mother's favourite thread.

It had become a good luck charm for her – it had led her to Saffron Vale, and her new life here, after all – and it was the only thing she had left of her mother apart from a few memories; a smile, the flutter of translucent wings, and snippets of half-remembered phrases.

Crimson brought the thread to her lips and kissed it, her eyes becoming teary as the loss of her mother struck her anew. It never went away, but sometimes it caught her unawares – like now – and those were always the worst times, when the grief bubbled through her, clutching at her heart like a thousand needles stabbing at once.

But she knew how to deal with it. Crimson allowed herself a few moments to acknowledge the loss and then she focused on the reason why she grieved; the love she had for her mother and that her mother had for her. She went through all the memories she had of their too short time together, smiling as she remembered what her mother said as they sorted through fabrics and threads together;

"Everything has its time. Each colour its perfect complement."

Back then, Crimson had been eager to help her mother and

had sat next to her, watching the needle dip in and out of the fabric. The transformation from flat material to finished garment had seemed like magic to young Crimson and still did.

She took a deep breath. "Thank you, mother. If you can hear me, I love you and please help me with these dresses." A lightness filled her, lessening the needles in her chest. For an instant, colours swirled about her and she felt in a different plane of existence. *Was this the aether?* It was beautiful. And it felt…well, she didn't know how to describe it. It was like dancing on air, like the soft brush of a first kiss, like a mother's embrace, like joy, deep and simple and wonderful and everywhere. Did everyone experience the aether like this? She had no comparison, but no wonder magic was revered. It was incredible.

As quickly as it had appeared, the twirling lightness vanished. Crimson took a breath and placed the thread back in her box with reverence before selecting a plain white silk thread for tacking the bodice together. For the neater finishing stitches, she would use a yellow that matched the saffron sunshine fabric, but with such an important dress, she was doing things by the book. Her old mentor would be proud.

Crimson hummed a tune as she threaded her needle, settled herself into the tailor's position – cross-legged, in a patch of sunlight – reached for the first set of pattern pieces and began sewing. As her fingers flew across the fabric, she wondered if a tiny piece of magic might make its way into the dress.

Foolishness. Crimson smiled at her wild imagination. But, still, just in case, she whispered, "Grant the wearer all her wishes for a happy life."

Chapter 20

~ *Rainbow River* ~

"Y OU NEED A BREAK." Lief loomed over Crimson and put his hand on the counter where she sat sewing.

"You're blocking my light."

"I haven't seen you all week."

"That's not true…" Crimson trailed off. Lief raised an eyebrow at her. Maybe it was true, but she had to put her best friend's wedding before…whatever it was she had with Lief.

"You're doing too much, Red, and you know what happens to the candle that burns at both ends."

"If I let you tell me, will you let me get on with this?"

"It burns out faster."

Crimson threw up her hands, abandoning her attempts at a

design for the invitations. "What do you suggest? There's too much to do and I have to do it all."

"Come with me."

"Didn't you hear what I said? There's too much to do."

"Give me an hour of your time and I'll leave you alone."

"Promise?"

Lief laughed and strode out of the shop. She sighed and rubbed her eyes. By the Artisan, she ought to stay. Once the invitation was finished, she needed to find some way to print however many were needed – a figure that was still growing. Plus, the dresses weren't finished; beading took forever. Not to mention screwing up the courage to ask Dilly and Duncan to do the wedding cake. Crimson sighed. In the scheme of all that, what was one hour away? At least then Lief would stop bothering her, and she knew from experience how persistent he could be.

"Come on, Smudge."

Crimson stomped out of her shop to find Lief leaning against the wall as if he knew she would come. Frustrating man. "Where are we going, then?"

Another laugh. "That's what I like about you, Red. You get straight to the point. Come on." He picked up a wicker basket by his feet and led the way out of town towards the river.

"The river?"

Lief glanced at the sky. "Come on, we'll miss it."

"What is so urgent that we have to go now?"

"You can't ever be silent, can you?"

Crimson narrowed her eyes and clamped her lips together. She was silent a lot of the time. After all, she worked alone in her workshop most evenings and weekends. Well, she wasn't going to say anything until they'd got wherever they were going. That would show him.

Lief kept walking, counting under his breath. Hah! It wasn't like he was quiet. Why was he counting, anyway?

"Why are you counting?" she blurted out.

"Less than a minute before you spoke."

Crimson ground her teeth. Infuriating man. "At least tell me where you're taking me."

"To the river."

Crimson stopped. "I've been to the river before. This is a waste of time."

"Trust me. You'll want to see this. But I'm not going to force you." He didn't break his stride, and Smudge stayed at his heels, leaving Crimson alone on the path.

She glanced back at the town before huffing and scurrying to catch up with him. "This had better be worth it," she muttered.

Lief kept that stupid grin on his face, like he had the best secret in the world, and carried on walking in silence.

He stopped on the riverbank, a little upstream from where she'd found Ovelia practicing holding her breath, poor girl. Speaking to her father had not gone well. *That was an understatement.* Crimson added 'speak to Pollonius and Greezi again' to her mental to do list.

Crimson looked around for something remarkable about this particular spot. Nothing. It was a patch of yellowing grass on part of the bank that jutted out a little farther into the river, but Lief rummaged in the basket and pulled out the worn tartan blanket that she remembered from his house and spread it on the ground.

Once it was flat, he plonked himself down and patted the spot next to him. "Sit."

Crimson flopped down next to him.

"Good girl."

"I'm not a dog."

He laughed and she found a small smile hovering on her lips. She enjoyed being with him, somehow all the tension she carried in her back and shoulders eased when she was near him and their banter soothed her soul.

"So, why are we here?"

"Any minute now…just eat and keep watching the river." Lief passed her a pasty. Still warm. Its residual heat seeped into her fingers as she took a bite, savouring the flaky pastry and the meaty contents of the half moon shaped local delicacy.

Crimson kept her eyes on the river. It was…a river. That was it. A sort of brownish colour that spoke of the sticky mud that lay beneath the surface. Crimson shuddered, her mind plunging back to her ill-fated attempt to rescue Ovelia that had almost led to her drowning.

Lief put his arm around her shoulders, lending her his reassuring body heat. He straightened and pointed. "There!"

"What?" Crimson squinted upstream in the direction he indicated. It still looked like a river…then she saw it. She gasped and leaned forward. *How was it possible?*

The river had turned into a literal rainbow with red through to violet flowing down in neat rows. Crawling to the edge of the bank, she gazed at her reflection in the violet stream nearest her and risked putting her fingers in, allowing the frigid water to trail past. "How?" she breathed as she gazed at the riot of colour flowing down the river.

Lief shrugged, his keen ears picking up on her whispered question. "Something to do with currents and the dyes. It happens about twice a year when the conditions are right."

"It's beautiful."

"Yes." There was a huskiness to Lief's voice that made her insides squirm in a pleasant way that she would have to analyse later, when she was back in the thick of her to do list. But, for now, she marvelled at the river, understanding finally how it got its name.

A huge fish leapt out of the water in a graceful arc. A flash of rainbow scales and a silver underbelly before it disappeared back into the river, splashing her face with indigo droplets.

"Rainbow trout," Lief said.

Less than a minute later the water returned to its former murky brown and Crimson sat back on the blanket.

"That was amazing. Thank you."

Lief shrugged like it was nothing instead of one of the most marvellous things she had ever seen, something that she would remember for the rest of her life.

"Red, there's something I've got to tell you." Lief coughed and looked away.

She put a hand on his chest. "You don't have to say anything." Crimson took a deep breath. "I misunderstood what happened with your sister." In retrospect, it was obvious, but she barrelled on, ignoring her stupidity. "And I'm sorry for punishing you for my misunderstanding."

Lief's lips pulled up at one corner and he opened his mouth to speak. Crimson kept going. If she didn't say anything now, she might never. "I like you. A lot."

"Like me like *like* like me?"

Crimson nodded and swallowed. "But…" She hated what she was about to do, but he deserved a proper relationship. He deserved someone who could put him first and be present. And she couldn't do that. Not right now. "There's so much to do with the wedding and I won't be present enough to be in a relationship. I can't be with you."

Chapter 21

~ A surprising response ~

CRIMSON'S HAND WAS STILL on Lief's chest, so she felt him tense as she rejected him before he'd had a chance to say anything. He stared out at the fast-flowing river, not speaking. Maybe she'd misunderstood, and he didn't have those sorts of feeling for her. She wouldn't blame him if he didn't. She'd spent so much time ignoring him and otherwise being rude that she might have pushed him away for good.

After an age, Lief spoke. "So you're saying you can't be with me right now?" There was a hint of pain under his forced lightness.

Crimson sagged with relief. He understood. "Yes."

"But you want to be with me."

"Yes," her voice was husky with feelings she'd barely let herself consider.

Lief nodded. "I can work with that."

"Thank you for understanding."

"I don't understand, not really." He leaned closer. "I don't understand why you didn't ask me who Bircha was instead of assuming the worst of us both. I don't understand how you can deny what's between us when it's burning me up so much that I can't think around you, and I don't understand why you want to put that aside instead of embracing it right here right now."

Crimson licked her lips. When he said it like that, he had a point.

"But if that's what you truly want, I'll try to understand, and I won't ask for anything more than friendship…not until after the wedding."

"Thank you," Crimson whispered, her chest aching from disappointment even though he had given her exactly what she wanted right now.

"We are still friends, right?"

"Of course." Crimson forced a smile onto her face to cover up whatever these emotions were that swirled around her stomach and heart, threatening to unravel her.

"Good. So you can let me help."

"What?" It was such a jump from what they had been talking about that Crimson felt dizzy.

"With the wedding. Ask for help."

"I should get back."

Lief took hold of her hand, still pressed to his muscled shirt. "This is the first break you've had since, when?"

"Since Ayla asked me to help," Crimson mumbled.

"And it's barely been an hour and you want to get back to work. You'll end up sick, or worse. Let me help. Let the town help. He's maire for all of Saffron Vale, for moon's sake."

"You really want to help?"

"Sometimes you are the most stubborn person I know, Red. And I grew up with Bircha. She decided to swim in the river when she was three."

"How did that go?"

"She nearly drowned. Four times, before she let me teach her in the bathing pools. Anyway, yes, I want to help. I don't want to watch the woman I care about more than the twin moons burn herself to nothing."

Crimson's heart swelled and her skin tingled. He cared about her. She'd known it but hearing him say it made her feel light inside and giddy as a whirling spindle.

"What are you grinning about, Red?"

"You just said you like me."

"If it makes you look at me like that, I'll say it as often as you want, but I might not be able to wait until after this moon forsaken wedding."

Crimson flushed.

"Are you sure you want to wait?"

She nodded, not trusting herself to speak because she might let her heart lead instead of her head and then her best friend's wedding might end up ruined. And Ayla meant the world to her. She would not let her best friend down. Not even for the joy and romance that Lief promised.

Lief sighed. "So, what can I do to lighten your burden?"

Chapter 22

~ Catering ~

CRIMSON GULPED DOWN HER fear as she cooled her heels outside Hambrosia – the butcher's shop owned by Greezi. She had managed to let go of a small selection of tasks on the wedding to do list after her conversation with Lief; his sister had taken charge of decorations with a fervour that surprised Lief so much he had asked if she were ill.

But Crimson had kept a lot of items on the list, and sorting the catering was one of them, as well as mending the rift between the ham and egg shop owners. So she hoped to catch two lobsters with one net as the saying went in Saffron Vale. Lief had offered to accompany her, but this was something she had to do alone.

Crimson squared her shoulders and strode into Hambrosia with what she hoped was an air of confidence. She stopped in the doorway, gaping at the scene until the door hit her as it swung shut.

"Greezi and Pollonius…"

They looked up from their conversation and stared at her.

"You're both here," Crimson finished weakly.

"Yes." Pollonius frowned. "I would say that was obvious."

"But…you hate each other?"

They both had the decency to look sheepish. Greezi cleared her throat. "Yes, we still have some unresolved differences. But we realised that, even though his great-great-grandmother was a lying witch–"

"And her great-great-grandfather was a thieving knave–"

"Quite." Greezi's voice tightened, and she continued, "But that was in the past and the actions of our ancestors of not dictate our present. So we decided to bury the hatchet."

"Really?" Crimson's eyes widened. "How…mature of you."

"Yes, I'm glad I had the idea," Pollonius said.

"You? I think you'll find this was my idea." A vein stood out in Greezi's neck.

Pollonius waved her away. "Regardless. We want to find a way to get on sufficiently so that our children don't leave the vale. I might not want to spend Lantern Night with her–"

"You couldn't keep up with an orc Lantern Night, dwarf!"

"Hah! Bring it on! I can outdrink and outparty any man, woman or *orc* in this vale!" Pollonius snatched up his mug and started chugging his drink down.

"That's coffee, you stupid dwarf."

Pollonius slammed his mug back on the counter and wiped his lips. "Hah! Beat you."

"You were saying," Crimson prompted, seeing Greezi's eyes narrow.

"As I was saying, we think we can come to civil terms so that our children don't feel they have to leave the vale."

"That is excellent news."

"Eggs-cellent! Hah! Well done, Miss Brouderer. Yet another reason eggs are superior to cooked meat; more puns."

"You were always too ham-bitious for your own good, Pollonius. There are plenty of meat-based jokes. For example, did you know that meat is another word for–"

"Alright, alright," Crimson interrupted before Greezi could finish her sentence. "Well, I'm pleased you've put the past behind you and can look forward because I have a favour to ask."

"How intriguing. Ask away. After all, it's thanks to you that we realised how stupid we have been. To think how we've wasted all these years, all these generations on pointless hatred."

Greezi rolled her eyes. "Let the woman talk."

"Right, yes, well I wanted to ask you to do the catering for the maire's wedding. Together."

The dwarf and the orc exchanged a look before Greezi nodded. "I think we can find a way to do that."

Pollonius held his hand up. "One moment. This is a monumental favour. Last I heard, the guest list topped over five hundred."

"It's at nearly a thousand now," Crimson said under her breath.

"You expect us to provide food for that many people, for free?"

"No, not at all. The maire is paying for everything."

Two sets of eyes lit up at that. Pollonius gave a slow smile and Crimson knew that the maire was about to get charged an exorbitant amount of money for ham and eggs. If it had been just his wedding, she might have allowed that, but her friend's happiness was on the line too. "I'm happy to negotiate on the couple's behalf once you've got a suggested menu."

The smiles didn't dull but Crimson's brightened. She was confident in her haggling skills and she would get her friend and the maire their money's worth. "Remember that there will be many dignitaries from across the queendom attending, so we want to show what Saffron Vale can do. I'm speaking to Dilly and her brother next about the cake and deserts so feel free to include them in the menu planning."

"We could create a unique dish that showcases the best of our vale, with eggs at the centre..."

"And ham! And saffron sauce…"

"Brilliant idea!"

"I'll leave you two to plan then," said Crimson.

The orc and dwarf waved her away as Greezi pulled out a sheaf of paper and a quill, while Pollonius outlined his ideas with his hands.

Chapter 23

~ *The cake* ~

OUTSIDE THE SHOP, OVELIA barrelled into Crimson and wrapped her arms around her. "Thank you, thank you."

Crimson patted her on the shoulder and looked to Hamlet, who stood behind his girlfriend – dwarffriend? – for help.

He beamed back and swept them both into an orc-sized hug. "I don't know how you did it, but they're actually talking to each other."

"It's amazing."

"Great," Crimson wheezed.

"Sorry." Hamlet let her down and Crimson rubbed her ribs.

"It feels so good not to have to hide our love anymore, doesn't it, Hammikins?"

Hammikins? Crimson kept her face still.

"Truly a weight off my chest, darling Ovelia. The freedom to declare my love for you any time I wish has fulfilled my every desire."

The dwarf blushed. "Surely not your every desire, love."

Hamlet laughed. Crimson raised her eyebrow.

"You have our unending gratitude, Crimson, and you'll be the first to be invited when we get married."

"You're getting married?"

"Not yet, but soon. I can't risk Dad changing his mind about approving of the match. He still glares at Hamlet every time he comes into the shop."

"Maybe that's a protective father thing?" Crimson was on shaky ground here. She didn't know who her father was, but she had read a lot of fictional fathers who hated any of their daughter's partners on instinct.

"Maybe, but better to act fast."

"We will strike while the iron is hot!"

"Hold that thought…" Crimson saw Milus leave the comfort of his forge and march across the street like a man on a mission. She left Hamlet and Ovelia staring into each other's eyes and wandered over to the Cozy Lobster café in time to see Ig leave. Milus padded over to him.

Crimson arrived in time to hear Milus say, "…go to the wedding with me?"

Ig blinked up at the large minotaur. "Oh no, no, no, no."

"No?" asked Milus.

"No?" repeated Crimson. "Excuse us one moment, I think he's a bit confused." She drew the tylluan to one side. "What are you doing? You like him. He's just asked you to the wedding. Say yes!"

"It's far too soon to go to a social event together. Look!" Ig pulled out his notebook. "Here, see, we should have gone on at least one date alone before going to an event together. And that's not the next step anyway!" He hooted miserably.

Crimson placed her hands on his shoulders. "Ig, you are the smartest person I know, but you are being remarkably stupid. Sometimes things don't go according to the rules that we write for ourselves or the books we follow. Sometimes life has other plans." The tylluan shook his head. "Sometimes you can skip a step."

He looked up at her with something like hope in his large eyes. "Skip a step?"

"Yes." She seized on the idea that seemed to be getting through to him. "Sometimes you can't follow rules. Sometimes you can add blue to make white."

He frowned. "Technically, that *is* following the rules of colour theory…but I think I take your point. So, I should say yes?"

"Yes!" She pushed his shoulder to spin him around and grinned up at Milus, who stood watching them.

"So, you will go with me?" the minotaur asked.

"Yes. I should very much like that."

Milus' face split into a broad smile. "Good."

"Good," repeated Ig.

"So, that's good," said Crimson. "I have to go speak to Dilly, will you two be alright?"

"I think so," said Milus.

Crimson waited until Ig agreed before leaving them both staring shyly at the ground. There must be something in the air today. She shook her head and entered the café, inhaling the sweet scent of chocolate mixed with the bitterness of coffee and the floral scent of tea.

"Crimson! What can I get you? I'm closing up, but I've got a cauliflower pasty left." Dilly gave her a cheerful smile from where she scrubbed a table, the yellow cloth in her hand contrasting with her purple skin.

Crimson's stomach growled at the reminder of food. With all the worry about the wedding, and the sewing, she hadn't eaten anything since morning. "Thank you."

Crimson rummaged in her pocket for some money, but Dilly waved away payment. "It'd only go to the gulls if you didn't take it."

"That's too kind, Dilly, but really, I have to give you something."

"Tell you what, I'll overcharge you next time, how about that?"

Crimson laughed and shook her head, knowing that Dilly wouldn't charge her extra, but she could leave a large tip to cover the pasty when she was next in.

"Was there anything else?" Dilly asked as she wiped down a table and placed the chairs upside down on top of it. "I've got the floor to mop."

"Actually…I wanted to talk to you about the wedding."

Dilly paused with a chair in midair. "What about it? I haven't seen an invite yet."

"The invites will be going out shortly. We've got an appointment with the printers this week." As long as the maire and Ayla made a decision, that would take one thing off the list.

"Right you are then." Dilly carried on cleaning tables and stacking chairs.

Crimson bobbed around in front of her. "I wanted to talk about the cake."

The petalborn froze and pursed her lips. "I thought Miss La-Dee-Da Baker would want to do her own cake, as she's such a fancy baker all the way from the big city."

"Please, Dilly, Ayla isn't like that. I think you'd like her if you gave her a chance."

"She said she wanted to open a bakery. Here. Like Duncan's baking isn't good enough for her and her hoity toity taste buds."

"What about the maire? You like him, don't you?"

Dilly shrugged her shoulders. "He's alright. A bit of a pill, and a pain on the planning committee, but he's got the vale's best interests at heart…but I can't support someone who wants to set up in competition to Duncan."

"And what does he think about it? Doesn't Duncan deserve the opportunity to make the cake of the year?" Crimson seized on Dilly's love for her brother. It was an underhand trick, perhaps, but desperate times called for desperate measures.

Dilly chewed the inside of her cheek.

"It would set him up, set both of you up. With Maire Bowan's connections, he could probably get you a write up in The Golden Acorn…"

Dilly rolled her eyes. "You don't need to over sugar the pudding, Crimson. I understand what you're saying." She sighed. "Give me fifteen minutes to close up and we'll go next door to see Duncan. But if he says no, it's no. Got it?"

Crimson nodded and grabbed a cloth. If she helped, then they could get done in record time. Dilly took her time, deliberately drawing out the close as she found more surfaces to clean, and insisted on mopping the floor twice, but soon there was nothing left to do and, with a grunt, she locked up and they both went next door to her brother's bakery.

Crimson repeated her request to Duncan, and Dilly couldn't resist mentioning that Ayla was a baker and if she moved to Woolton, she'd set up her own shop and ruin Duncan's trade. Brother and sister exchanged a long, silent look while

Crimson shifted from foot to foot, her hands gripped tight in front of her.

If they said no, she didn't know any other bakers in Saffron Vale, apart from Ayla. And she couldn't ask her friend to make the cake for her own wedding, not when she already had so much to think about. Perhaps Crimson could learn to bake. She dismissed that idea as Plan Z. Crimson couldn't boil an egg, much less make even the simplest of cakes, and Ayla deserved the best. Maybe she could travel to another vale and ask the baker there.

After an interminable silence, Duncan gave a short nod and Dilly sighed. "What do they have in mind?"

Chapter 24

~ *The invites* ~

CRIMSON HELD UP TWO pieces of paper for the happy couple to look at.

Ayla squinted at them. "They both look white."

Smudge cocked his head to one side as if contemplating the choices.

"This one is an egg white, and this one is daisy," Crimson said, shaking the paper at them.

"Is white the right colour?" asked the maire, stroking his beard. "Perhaps yellow would work better with the theme."

"If you have yellow paper, it's harder for the ink to show up. But what about a crème paper?" Crimson rummaged through the stack of samples. "Here. And this comes in the thick paper you liked so much, Ayla."

Ayla rubbed the new sample between her fingers. "I think the thickness lends it extra weight."

"I quite agree with you darling; it adds a certain gravitas."

"It won't match with the linens you chose for the napkins." Crimson twirled the card between her fingers. "But I don't suppose anyone's going to compare the invites with the serviettes."

"Then we'll take it," said the maire. "Are we finished with the invites?"

"We still need to agree the wording and the font choices. I've arranged for us to go to Ig's lighthouse now. Oh, and I need the final list of names."

The maire struck his head with the palm of his hand. "That reminds me, there are a few more people I'd like to invite."

"How many?" Crimson's grip on the card tightened, denting the sample.

"Just another dozen or so."

Crimson handed over the wedding book and told the maire to write them down before they went to peruse the styles of writing available.

This meant travelling to Ig's lighthouse, where he had his own personal stamping table for making prints. The maire's office had one as well, but the choice of fonts there was limited to boring, official letters for making proclamations, whereas Ig had promised her a better choice more suitable for weddings.

They took the paper sample with them, and Ayla walked in between the maire and Crimson, linking her arms through theirs. Smudge gambolled along happily at their feet, stopping to sniff interesting street corners and puddles.

Crimson sneezed.

"Are you coming down with something?" Ayla asked, all concern and sympathy.

"No, it's probably just the breeze. There's a bit of stale shellfish in it, don't you think?"

The maire took a deep breath. "Bracing, isn't it? Classic Saffron Vale air. Nothing like it in all the queendom. I daresay Juniper Vale doesn't have anything like this."

Ayla nodded and took her own, not quite so deep, breath. Crimson agreed with the maire. The fresh mountain air that surrounded Juniper Vale was nothing like this coastal assault on the nostrils. It was the one thing she hadn't got used to in the vale yet. Maybe she never would. Maybe only people born here didn't notice the briny tang and the weird aftersmell of something fishy that never quite went away.

Crimson sneezed twice more on the way to Ig's house, and by the time they got inside, her throat was sore. No doubt from the increasing air pressure as they climbed the path to the red and white striped lighthouse.

The door to the main room on the ground floor was open, so Crimson climbed the few steps and went inside with Ayla and the maire following.

"Ig? Ig? Are you here?" No answer. "We're here for the printing options. Ig?"

A crash sounded from somewhere in the room, but there was no sign of the tylluan among the debris that littered the floor and every available work surface.

A small face popped up with enormous eyes.

"Aaah!" Crimson jumped backwards before realising it was Ig wearing some goggles. She placed her hand over her fluttering heart. "You scared me."

Smudge bounded over, ever hopeful that people might give him treats. Ig didn't disappoint and fished a biscuit out of a dented tin for the small dragon.

"Hmm? Oh sorry, I wanted to calibrate the doohickeys before you got here, and time must have got away from me. Now, take a seat and I'll find the letters. They're around here somewhere…" He turned his head from left to right and almost all the way round as his keen eyes searched for the letters.

Ayla perched on a rocking chair with a mechanism made of wooden sticks looming above it. Thick mustard yellow yarn looped around the sticks and Ayla looked up nervously as the sticks clacked together in time with the slight rocking motion of the chair. "What is it?" she asked, not taking her eyes off the moving needles.

"That? A knitting machine. I thought that even relaxing time can be productive."

"Ingenious!" the maire exclaimed. "This could revolutionise the clothing industry! Have you patented it?"

"The only thing I can get it to knit reliably is a scarf and it can't tie it off at all so that has to be done manually. Do you want it when it's finished? It can go to any length you like. The only real problem is when it gets so long that it tickles the top of your head, which rather distracts from anything else you might be doing. I wonder if I could adjust the frame so it leads off to one side…" Ig moved towards the machine.

"Maybe later?" suggested Crimson. If Ig got caught up in tinkering with one of his inventions, they would never get the invitations agreed.

"Yes, of course. Here is the stamping table or you may know it as a small printing press." Ig pulled a dust sheet off a large contraption that stood against one wall of the circular room. "Now we just need to find the lettering…" He bent to dig around in another pile of boxes which wobbled precariously as he searched.

"Did that table just move?" Crimson narrowed her eyes at the mechanical device that Ig claimed was a printing press.

"What?" Ig gave it a worried glance. "No. Why would a stamping table move? Ha, Ha. What a thought."

Crimson didn't have an answer to that, but she kept a close eye on the table that may or may not be able to move by itself.

"Aha!" Ig pulled out a box near the bottom of the pile, sending the rest of the boxes clattering to the floor. He cleared another surface by sweeping a stack of papers to the floor and laid out the neat box of letters. "Each of these layers is a different style of writing from chunky gothic to swirly copperplate to this angular square font which combines readability with shapes."

"What's this one?" Crimson pulled a small piece of metal with a bird cut out from it.

"That is actually very interesting. You see, my good friend Leoninus and I worked on a cipher that combines pictures and shapes to allow complicated messages to be sent without the need for letters at all. We based it on some engravings found in the ruins at–"

"I don't think we want them. Our guests will need a decoder to read the invites."

"Well yes, it only works if both of you know the code, but it would be a novel idea. No one else would have an invitation like it."

"Like a puzzle to solve before people can come." The maire's eyes shone.

"But there isn't time for people to crack a code," Crimson said, her voice breaking, "we can't even send the invites until we know the date of the harvest, assuming that's still when you want to have the wedding?" The maire and Ayla nodded, confirming that was still their chosen date as Crimson cleared her throat. "And if Ig shares his code, then his messages won't be secret anymore."

Ig gave a small hoot of concern. "That is something I had

not considered. Perhaps I could come up with a new, unique cipher for the wedding. It might take me some time…"

"Oh well, let's discard that idea then. Too bad. Now do any of these other letters grab you?" Crimson handed one to Ayla.

"These letters are all backwards," said Ayla. looking at a complicated 'S' layered with swirls and flourishes.

"Ah, well that's the thing of it. For a print to appear the right way for us to read, you have to have the letters back to front on the stamps." Ig hooted and rubbed his hands together.

"What if our missive contains more than one of the same letter?"

"I've worked out an algorithm for the most likely letters based on our usage in day-to-day writing, so these boxes contain the perfect amount of letters for ninety-five per cent of printing you can get on a single page."

"What's the other five per cent?" asked Crimson.

"Well, if you wanted something with a lot of 'z's perhaps. But no matter, because in those cases, I can double print to fill in the missing letters. It's all a case of configuration. So, what do you want the invite to say?"

After a long discussion and much editing, Ayla and the maire agreed on the following wording for the invite in the swirly letters:

Jollivity Cuthbert Bowan

and

Ayla Sourcrust

Joyfully invite you to celebrate

their wedding

at two o'clock on

"We won't know the date until the Great Lobster tells us the harvest parameters."

"No matter, I can print up the invites and add the date in later," Ig said, pausing as he took down the letter blocks.

At the beach near the lighthouse,

Followed by a slap-up meal in the saffron fields.

Wear something yellow.

RSVP ASAP c.o. The Maire's Office, Woolton, Saffron Vale .

"You really want to say 'slap-up meal' in your wedding invitation?" asked Crimson, peering over Ig's shoulder.

"What else should we call it?" asked the maire.

"Ooo, ooo, how about 'a fabulous party'," said Ayla.

"Yes, or 'raucous celebration'," said the maire.

"On second thoughts, slap-up meal is fine."

Chapter 25

~ Crimson gets sick ~

CRIMSON CURLED UP IN bed that night with a mug of tea to soothe her sore throat and the cough that had developed from nowhere. She did not have time to be sick. Crimson repeated that mantra until she fell asleep.

It didn't work.

The following morning, she awoke feeling as if a razor blade had lodged itself in her throat and she was both too hot and too cold.

"I don't have time for this." She spoke out loud as if that would stave off whatever illness she had contracted. Crimson instantly regretted her speech as her throat burned with every word.

Smudge jumped down from his place on the bed and looked

at her with large amber eyes.

With a moan, she sat up and swung her feet out of bed, stumbling on the floor. With her eyes half shut and slow movements, she made it to the back door, where she let out the dragon. Crimson managed to pour him some breakfast. She couldn't face food for herself right now. Crimson considered the kettle for a long time before deciding it wasn't worth it, and she needed to get to work.

She unlocked the front door of the shop and opened the shutters while she was downstairs. Saving energy was important when she felt so awful. Then she crawled back upstairs, pulled on her comfiest dress, and grabbed the bodice of Ayla's wedding gown.

There was so much work to do before the first dress fitting and she could not afford to be sick. And that was before she thought about everything else that needed doing; she had to get the guest list to Ig for the invites so he would know where to send them, arrange a special express postal delivery when they finally had the dates so that the guests from the farthest corners of the queendom had a chance to get there, sort the flowers, arrange transport to the beach and then from the beach to the fields for the reception, sort a marquee for the reception, and music, and rings….the list went on and on.

Crimson's head reeled just thinking about it and she wobbled as she went downstairs, clutching the bodice and her sewing box to her chest.

She set up behind the counter and hoped that no one would

decide to come in today. If she didn't have to interact with anyone, she could focus on the bodice.

Crimson opened her sewing box and blinked as the threads in their neat rows swam in front of her eyes. She took twice as long as usual to select the sunshine yellow thread that matched the fabric and the needle wobbled as she attempted to thread it. Maybe if she rested her eyes for a moment, just until everything stopped spinning and her head ceased pounding.

The bell on the shop door rang, jolting Crimson awake. "I wasn't asleep."

Lief smiled at her. "Yes, you were."

"Why are you here?" Crimson squinted up at him. *Why was the sun so bright?*

"You're ill." Lief's voice was laced with accusation.

"Am not."

"Are too." Were there two of him?

"I just need to finish this." Crimson blinked at the bodice. What was she meant to do? It felt like her head was full of wool scraps.

"You've worked yourself too hard and now you're ill."

"And you get to say, 'I told you so'. Is that why you're here?" Crimson dissolved into a coughing fit that almost made her fall from her seat.

"I'm here because I wanted to make sure you were eating and Ig told me you were looking peaky."

"It's not your job to take care of me," said Crimson when she could talk again. It came out as a croak.

"I want to."

"I'm fine."

He turned to the door, waved at someone outside, and called them in. "Ayla!"

"Oh no," said Crimson.

The elf burst through the door with a headache-inducing jangle of the shop bell. "Morning Lief, Crimson. Burned crusts, but you look awful. What's the matter?"

"Nothing."

"She's worked herself ragged running around trying to do everything for your wedding."

Ayla rushed to Crimson's side and placed a cool hand on her forehead.

"Mmm, that feels nice."

"You're burning up," Ayla said. "Oh Crimson, why didn't you say something?"

"I'm fine."

"I thought you wanted to do all this. I know you love being in control, but you should say if it's too much."

"Just want you to be happy."

"You working yourself to death does not make me happy," Ayla scolded. "Now, I'm going to make you some tea and broth and you are going to bed."

"Can't sleep. Must work."

"No, you don't!" Ayla moved Crimson's sewing out of reach. "You are going to bed and, when you are better, we will talk about what needs to be done for the wedding and I will sort it. It's not too late, I can get someone else to make the dress."

"No!" Crimson grabbed for the bodice. This was her masterpiece, laced with love for her friend. Tears pricked behind her eyes. "You don't want me to make your wedding dress?"

"I want you to get better."

"I will." Crimson nodded. "But please, I want to make this for you."

"Alright. But when you feel better, you will accept some help with other parts of the wedding so you can focus on the things only you can do, like the wedding dress." Ayla folded her arms and gave Crimson a hard look. "Deal?"

"Deal." Crimson hung her head and let Ayla lead her upstairs to bed where she slept for twenty-four hours straight.

Chapter 26

~ *A dwarf with an anvil* ~

A LOUD THUMPING WOKE Crimson. It took her a long while to realise that the banging wasn't coming from her head and was someone at the door.

She staggered from her cosy bed and made her way downstairs. She hadn't planned to open today, in fact, she hadn't planned on doing much of anything except recovering from whatever illness plagued her.

Crimson paused in the kitchen, taking in the flask left on the table with a handwritten note from Lief.

Drink it. Don't argue, Red.

Her lips curved into a smile at his grumpy words. She unscrewed the lid and sniffed. Mmmm. Some sort of broth. Her mouth watered. When had she last eaten?

The thumping continued.

"I'm coming," she croaked. A small figure kept up the pounding so as Crimson opened the door, they almost walloped her in the chest. Crimson jumped back.

"Thank the Artisan. I was about to jump right back on the cart and head home."

"Lisa? What are you doing here?"

The dwarf bustled past her, lugging a bag after her. Something inside it clinked as it dragged on the floor. "You asked me for some rings for a wedding. You can't make rings without seeing the couple, and you didn't include the sizes, and you said it was urgent, so I thought I'd come to you."

"But…your shop? Aren't you in the Capital?"

"Yes, and going so well that I can leave it for a little while. I'm not stopping, mind, just doing this job then heading straight back. I've left the kids with the mother-in-law, and she doesn't think there's any such thing as too much sugar."

"I didn't know you were married."

Lisa laughed. "I wasn't when we met, but," she blushed and her dark eyes shone, "I met someone in the city. Here, I made the rings for our wedding so you can see my work." She held up her hand and twisted it back and forth so Crimson could see the delicate leaves encircling a small diamond.

"It's beautiful."

"My best work." After a wistful sigh, the dwarf snapped to business. "Now, where can I set up my workbench?"

"Er…"

"Outside might be best, there's some fumes."

"I have a courtyard." That sounded too fancy for the paved patch of ground at the back of the shop.

"Perfect. And I'll need to meet the couple."

~

One hastily arranged meeting later and Lisa had listened carefully as bride and groom-to-be talked about their interests, the theme of the wedding and their love of Saffron Vale. Lisa nodded and sketched and when she was satisfied, shooed them all away while she set up her bench, complete with small anvil, on the paving slabs outside Crimson's shop.

She was there now, banging away, filing, melting, fiddling and doing whatever it was jewellers did as she sculpted the rings. Crimson squinted out of the door, taking her time putting away the plates from earlier. *Was that a third pair of glasses?* Each time she peeked out, the dwarf seemed to have more lenses in front of her eyes. A shower of sparks made Crimson jump back, pulling her long skirt away from any stray embers.

Smudge made to run outside, his long tongue licking at the

air, eager to take part in this new game. Crimson tried to keep him in, but the wily dragon slipped past her arms and danced around Lisa's feet.

"Sorry," Crimson said, hurrying to catch him while one hand kept her skirt pressed tight to her body.

"No worries, I'm done. Do you want to see?"

Crimson nodded. She leaned forward and gasped. Sat cooling on the bench were two perfect gold rings moulded into the shape of intertwining crocuses, or should that be crocii? "They're beautiful."

"Don't go losing them now." Lisa touched the cooling metal, nodded to herself and placed the rings into a velvet box which she tied with a ribbon and handed to Crimson before packing up her equipment.

"How much do I owe you?"

"It was a favour." Lisa straightened and looked Crimson straight in the eye. "You did me a great kindness in Innton. I don't forget it."

"It was nothing."

"It was everything after a hard day with my babies ready to collapse."

"And you've come all this way. You've more than repaid any favour you owed me. I insist on paying you for your work."

Lisa twisted her head to the side until her neck popped. "Alright." She took out a piece of paper and scribbled a figure on it.

"That isn't enough."

"Friends discount." Lisa grinned.

Crimson counted out the coins and added some extra, knowing that the maire wouldn't begrudge a few extra silvers for these bespoke rings. "Will you stay for the night?"

Lisa shook her head. "I want to get back as soon as possible. I paid the carter to wait for me."

"A meal, then?"

"We-ell," she stroked her long plait, "I wouldn't say no to some stargazey pie."

Chapter 27

~ *The dress fitting* ~

"I'M HERE FOR MY fitting," Ayla called from the doorway to the shop.

Crimson smiled and hurried over to hug her friend. "Everything's upstairs. You get started and I'll be up in a minute." She lowered her voice. "Are you wearing the underwear that you're going to wear for the big day? It's important, so the fit is right."

Ayla leaned forward with mischief in her eyes. "Who says I'm wearing underwear?"

Crimson blinked, not sure what to say in response. Her friend had certainly got saucier since her engagement to the maire.

Ayla swatted her on the arm. "I'm joking. And yes, I'm

wearing what I plan to wear for my wedding, like you told me yesterday…and the day before that…oh yes, and last week…and–"

"Alright, alright. Go on then."

With a laugh, Ayla disappeared through the kitchen and up the stairs to Crimson's bedroom-cum-workspace while Crimson finished her line of stitches over a patch for a pair of braies. She tucked the needle into the fabric so she could find it later and hurried upstairs to help her friend.

Stitches, she hoped that Ayla loved the dress. She had spent hours toiling over tulle and satin to create something sophisticated that matched the saffron theme of the wedding. Crimson smiled as she thought about Ayla's reaction to the small glittering beads she'd added to the fabric for a touch of sparkle under the glowing lights of the evening party. Normally confident in her creations, Crimson's hands trembled as she mounted the steps. What if Ayla hated it? What if she wasn't good enough to make a wedding dress?

While she'd spent her apprenticeship making bespoke upmarket gowns in Guilder Senda's Emporium, Crimson had only ever put the finishing touches to wedding dresses where Senda had wanted her neat stitches; she had never designed a wedding gown from start to finish.

Crimson's voice caught as she called to her friend, "I'm coming up. Are you decent?"

"This dress is amazing, Crimson. Where do you get your ideas from?"

Crimson crested the stairs and froze. Instead of the gorgeous pale green gown with the yellow bodice she had fashioned for her friend, Ayla had stepped into the dress on the other mannequin. The one she'd designed for Sibby's performance.

"What does this do?" Ayla tugged at the tab on the full netted lace skirt.

"No! It's not ready…" Crimson trailed off. Her friend had already ripped off the skirt to reveal the smaller, leaf green skirt beneath.

Ayla pointed her long legs. "How did you think of this? It's brilliant! I'm going to have to shorten my underdress."

Crimson took a deep breath and joined Ayla in front of the long mirror. "No, it's for–" She stopped as she took in Ayla's beaming face, the way her friend looked herself up and down in the mirror, turning to appreciate the fit and the way it emphasised the few curves she had.

"You've been a bit generous with my bust, but I love it." Ayla leaned forward and pulled Crimson into a hug. "I knew you were brilliant, but this is another level of genius." When Ayla released Crimson, the elf's eyes brimmed with tears. "Jojo is going to love it and no one will expect that it's really two dresses. Does the top come off too?" Ayla pulled at the structured bustier top.

"No!" Crimson pulled Ayla's hands away from the dress before she ruined the pearl beading on the bodice. She met Ayla's gaze. "Are you sure this is what you want? You wouldn't prefer something simpler? More nature based?" Crimson rushed to the other mannequin and pushed it closer to her friend.

Ayla bit her lip and reached a hand out to the green dress. "I like the way you've made the skirt look like leaves, but it's a bit understated. You shouldn't have made me two options though, Crimson. It must have taken you ages! You're the best. What's wrong? You look upset."

Stitches. Her best friend knew her too well. Crimson forced her lips to smile. "Nothing. I guess I just really liked the green dress. I could bead that top too and cover up the satin." Crimson's fingers twitched at the thought. It was almost criminal to cover the luscious fabric, but if her friend wanted glamour, she would do it.

Ayla stroked the fabric again, then went back to admiring her reflection. Crimson let out a soft sigh. Her friend had made her choice and was happy. She grabbed her pot of pins and knelt down at Ayla's feet. "Let's get this fitted, shall we?"

She would have to do something else for Sibby.

As if on cue, the bell rang and a familiar purr filled the shop, floating up to Crimson's workroom. "Darrling, I'm here for my fitting."

Stitches! Sibby was early.

Chapter 28

~ *Sibby and Ayla* ~

"**D**O WE HAVE A date yet, darrlings? I've promised to be in the Capital for a series of Lantern Night shows." Sibby fluttered one hand, pausing to admire her painted claws.

Ayla twisted her hands together. "Jojo wants to do it at the end of the saffron harvest."

"Which is?"

Ayla slumped onto Crimson's bed. "I don't know!" she wailed and lay down, covering her face with one of Crimson's patchwork silk pillows.

"Ayla, it'll be fine." Crimson lay next to her friend and pulled her into a hug. The cushion fell onto the quilt.

"It won't be fine. I have so much to do. Dilly hates me. I don't even know when the wedding is, and we haven't got the rings, or the flowers sorted. And I don't know how much anything costs! Jojo won't let me look at the accounts in case I get worried about the expense. I mean, I know he's wealthy thanks to all the saffron, but this wedding is huge."

"We can fix all of that." Crimson patted her back, hoping that was true.

"Really?" Ayla gazed up at Crimson.

"What are you always telling me?"

"That you're brilliant?"

Crimson threw a pillow at Ayla. "No! That there are more important things than money."

"I am very wise."

Sibby coughed. "This is all very sweet, darrrlings, but we need a date, and that dress needs a total revamp."

"Don't sugarcoat it for me," mumbled Crimson.

"What's all that noise out in the street?" Ayla threw open the window, letting in the breeze and the stiff scent of salt and gone off fish that hung around the coastal vale.

"The Great Lobster's here!" a voice floated up to them.

Crimson leaned out of the window next to her friend and saw the trail of people heading down towards the beach. "Looks like we'll have a date for the saffron harvest."

~

The trio headed down to the beach, following the crowd as the citizens of Saffron Vale went to hear what the Great Lobster had to say. They were towards the back of the crowd, but, using a combination of Ayla's name and position as the maire's fiancée and Crimson's small size, they weaved their way through to join the maire at the water's edge.

"Ayay, you made it! Allow me to present to you the Great Lobster, guardian of this fair vale since time immemorial, and my personal friend." He waved to a large rock formation coated with barnacles.

The rock formation moved.

"Lobby," the maire patted the lobster on its cratered shell. If it was possible for a lobster to roll its eyes, Crimson thought it would have. "Allow me the very great pleasure of introducing my fiancée, Ayla Sourcrust. She's the elf who finally tied this old goat down."

"A pleasure to meet you, Miss Sourcrust," the lobster said, his voice sounding like rocks tumbling together.

"Likewise." Ayla curtsied. "I do hope you can make it to our wedding."

"That depends on the date of the nuptials," the lobster burbled in a voice that reverberated over the cliffs. "I have promised Ig that I'll help with his latest foray into measuring the depth of the sea, but I'm sure we can push that back."

"And that depends on what you're about to tell us, Lobby."

The maire patted the lobster's shell. "We have our hearts set on wedding at the end of the saffron harvest."

"Ah, well in that case," the Great Lobster cleared their throat with a sound like pebbles rolling together, "citizens of Saffron Vale, I come with glad tidings. A great squall is coming so batten down your hatches the day after tomorrow, but after that the time will be ripe for the planting and growing of the saffron crocuses, which can be safely harvested in four to six weeks' time."

"This is glad tidings indeed. Ayla, my sweet, we can be wed as soon as the harvest is complete." Maire Bowan pulled Ayla down for a kiss.

Hardy, the town clerk ever present at the maire's side, cleared his throat pointedly. "May I suggest eight weeks to allow some contingency?"

"You know best, I'll leave it to you to sort the details, Hardy."

The clerk's eyes shone. "And the harvest?"

"Now, citizens of Saffron Vale, you have heard from our guardian. Prepare for the harvest, and my wedding!"

The clerk stepped forward, his voice clear. "Anyone with a plough team, please come to the fields straight away so we can prepare. Then, as soon as the storm's blown out, we can plant the bulbs."

"Good man," the maire clapped Hardy on the back.

The townsfolk dispersed with murmurs of excitement

around the upcoming harvest. Ig mentioned a upgraded clod crusher machine that he was certain would speed up the ploughing of furrows and turning the ground.

Crimson closed her eyes, listing all the tasks that she still had to do before the wedding; make Ayla's wedding dress look more showy for Sibby, make Sibby's dress look more bridal for Ayla, get the invites sent now they had a date…the list went on. At least the catering and the cake were sorted. Stitches, what about a marquee?

"Are you quite alright?"

Crimson opened her eyes to find she was alone next to the Great Lobster. "Yes, I'm fine, just lost in thought."

"It's just that everyone else is leaving."

"I should join them."

"You are troubled. I can feel it in my antennae."

"It's nothing."

"If you say so. But sometimes one must take a break to keep going."

Crimson's brow furrowed. "That makes no sense."

"Have you heard the story about the lobster and the blunt claw?"

"No."

"Once upon a time, there was a great lobster who had the sharpest claws in the sea. They were much sought after for their ability to slice through almost anything and agreed to help with the kelp farms at the bottom of the ocean.

"On the first day, they cut through half an acre's worth of debris, clearing the way for the kelp. Enthused, they returned and cut another third of an acre, and on the following day, a quarter until by the end of the week the lobster could barely cut through an eighth of an acre of detritus.

"Now this lobster was much upset by the falling progress and so spoke to a wiser, older great lobster and told them of their frustrations. The older lobster listened and nodded along and replied, 'What did you expect would happen? For you never took time to sharpen or care for your claws'."

Crimson waited, but it appeared that was the end of the story.

"Do you understand?" the Great Lobster asked.

"No."

"You have to take time to take care of your tools, whether that's a claw." The Great Lobster raised their enormous claw and clacked it twice to demonstrate. "Or whether that's your body and mind."

"Like how you can't cut fabric with blunt scissors."

"Yes, if that's the analogy you prefer. Now speaking of self-care, I shall have to get debarnacled for the maire's wedding. Toodle-oo." With that, the lobster edged backwards and disappeared into the surf.

Crimson watched them leave. Take care of herself. That was a novel idea. It was something Lief had told her to do, but what did it mean? "What does it mean to take care of yourself?"

"That's not normally a difficult question." Lief's voice made Crimson jump. For a large man, he could move quietly

Crimson acted how she always did when she was flustered around Lief, by lashing out. "How would you take care of yourself?"

He lifted one eyebrow at her.

"For self-care?" she asked again, attempting to clarify her unintended double entendre.

The corner of his lips twitched before his face softened and he answered. "I'd probably go for a walk, be out in nature for a bit, somewhere where I feel I can be myself, where I can run free and wild. What about you?"

"I don't even know how to think about answering that." Crimson sighed. What was wrong with her that she couldn't even decide what self-care meant?

"Close your eyes."

It was Crimson's turn to raise an eyebrow.

"Trust me."

Crimson bit her lip, but she did trust Lief. That was part of the problem, part of the allure he held for her. He would never let her down or take advantage of her. She closed her eyes.

"Now, think about having a day to yourself–"

"Hah!"

"This is imagination. Anything is possible. So you have a day where you don't have to get up early, where you have nowhere to be and nothing to do. No one is relying on you for anything. There's no work. What would you choose to do?"

Crimson took a deep breath. "I would…stay in bed reading. No. I'd take my design book and go for a walk, and I'd stop for a picnic somewhere with all my favourite foods; chocolate cake, one of Duncan's venison pies, a breaded egg. And then, when it got colder, I'd go home and light a fire and read a book."

"What type of book?" Lief asked.

"Is that important?"

"It's better for your imagination if you can be specific."

"A book on sewing."

"Really? To relax you'd read a book about the thing you do all day every day?"

Crimson blushed and curled her hands into nervous fists. "Alright, fine. A cosy romance book, something with a guaranteed happy ever after, where everything works out. Happy now?" Crimson opened her eyes and glared at Lief, daring him to laugh at her.

"Are you happy? That's the point."

"Let's just go. I've got too much to do."

Lief stood to one side and gave her a mock bow. "After you."

Crimson strode past him, feeling like she'd failed some sort of test. She turned back to say sorry when something in the sea caught her eye.

"Wait, was that a foam sprite?" Crimson twisted around to peer into the waves that lapped playfully at the seashore.

Lief shrugged. "They're always round here."

"I want to catch one. Maybe it can tell me if the wedding will be a success."

"You don't need a foam sprite to tell you that. Anything you set your mind to is a success. Look at your shop, your guild membership. What more do you want?"

"I want Ayla to be happy."

"And what about your happiness?" Lief asked, moving closer.

Crimson swallowed. "My happiness isn't important right now. It's Ayla who matters."

Lief's eyes glittered with something she couldn't place; maybe it was disappointment, maybe frustration, but he turned from her and stomped into the sea until it covered his bare feet. "You don't catch foam sprites, you ask them nicely."

Crimson watched him in silence. There was so much she wanted to say; that he mattered to her, that she wanted to be with him, but she couldn't commit right now. She longed to pull him close and feel his arms around her, but that wasn't fair, because she had no time. She had nothing to give in the mounting spectacle of the wedding preparation and she wouldn't start a relationship like that. It wasn't fair to him.

She'd been the person who had pined after another only to see their feelings ignored and then tossed aside. She wouldn't do that to someone else.

Instead of talking, she shucked off her emerald green boots, hiked up her skirts and headed into the water in search of a foam sprite.

Chapter 29

~ *Foam Sprites* ~

CRIMSON SPLASHED THROUGH THE surf and shivered as the freezing tide climbed higher up her legs. She made her way towards a group of sprites with shimmering wings and skin in different shades of watery aquamarine running from pale teal to deep blue.

"Excuse me!" she said. "What's the phrase? Hear my call and grant my wish so that the future I might enthrall? That doesn't sound right."

"No one will hear you over the waves. Excuse me! Hear her plea and grant her wish so that the future she might see." Lief bellowed, his voice carrying far over the sea. So those were the words.

He bent down and scrabbled under the surface until he found

some small pebbles which he tossed towards the sprites.

"You'll hurt them!"

"They like interesting rocks and things. I'm helping."

The foam sprites skipped over the tips of the waves, jumping in and out of the sea and ignoring the two people yelling.

"What do you know about it?"

"I'm only a warden. It's only my job to know about the creatures in the vale but sure, you go ahead, talk to a foam sprite yourself." He stalked back to shore and began picking through the flotsam and jetsam that lay on the beach.

Crimson lifted her skirt higher and tucked it into her belt. The sprites preferred the larger waves, riding the foamy bubbles down before heading back out to catch the next wave. Crimson could see the appeal. It looked fun; the sprites certainly laughed as they tumbled through the foamy swell. If the sea hadn't been the approximate temperature of an ice box, then she might be tempted to join them.

Crimson waded further in, aiming to meet the sprites on their turf, or surf, if you will. Her foot tripped over a concealed rock, and she tumbled into the sea with a shriek.

Water crashed over her, soaking her in a confusing swirl of salty waves and forcing her under. Her bottom hit the seabed with a gentle thump, and Crimson sat up, ready to claw her way out of the ocean. She broke the surface and gulped in a sweet breath of salty air.

"Do you want some help?" Lief took a step towards her, but

Crimson held up her hand.

Now her panic was over, it was easy to see that the water wasn't deep. A few of the sprites stopped their frolicking and bent over double in laughter at her antics. Crimson tested her ankle, circling it back and forth under the water. No matter, only her pride was hurt.

"Are you alright?" a tiny voice came from behind her.

Crimson turned and didn't see the large wave that slammed into her, sending her back under and forcing water up her nose. When it passed, she spluttered out the briny water, trying not to think about how fish went to the toilet in the ocean.

This time she stood up, her soaking dress hugging her body and her hair dripping fat water droplets into the sea.

"That looked like it hurt. Are you alright?" That voice again.

Crimson squinted, clearing the water from her eyes and her gaze came to rest on a tiny foam sprite barely larger than her hand who danced on the waves closer to the shore. The tiny humanoid wore a robe fashioned from sea kelp in a brackish tone that suited their midnight blue skin tone.

"I'm fine, thank you. More embarrassed than hurt. The sea was more powerful than I expected."

"It is," agreed the sprite. "I love the ocean, she's my home, but she's a fickle mistress. That's why I prefer being closer to shore. She's more honest when you can see the sand and rocks, it's the depths you have to take care with. She hides much under the waves." The sprite's gaze moved beyond Crimson to the vast ocean that spread out across the horizon, a dark grey-blue against the darkening sky.

Crimson shivered but didn't move out of the sea. This foam sprite had decided to speak with her, and she didn't want to do anything to break the spell.

"Why are you in the sea? I don't know much about big 'uns but don't you normally wear less when you go swimming?" The foam sprite sat on the wave and looked Crimson up and down with frank curiosity.

"I didn't want to go swimming, actually. This was a spur of the moment thing." Crimson took a breath. "I wanted to speak to a foam sprite."

"Well," the sprite rubbed her neck, "falling over and nearly drowning yourself in less than a foot of water is an unusual tactic, but you got my attention. What did you want to talk about?"

"Well, I heard that you can tell the future."

"Oh, that." The sprite sighed.

"Sorry, have I said something wrong?"

"Hmm? Oh no, it's just that any time I speak to a big 'un, all they want to know is the future. No one wants to actually talk to me and answer my questions."

"Oh." Crimson shifted in the water. "What sort of questions?"

"Just simple things, like, why can't you walk on water?

What is that building up there? Where do the bright colours come from in the river? But does anyone have time for that? No. They just want their future told."

"Maybe I can answer some of them."

"Really?" The sprite tiptoed along the waves, moving closer to Crimson.

"Yes. I don't know the answers to all of them, but I can try." She coughed. "First, I can't walk on water because I'm too heavy. I just sink."

The sprite giggled as Crimson splashed in the sea, demonstrating that she couldn't walk on the waves like the foam sprites.

"That building is the lighthouse. My friend Ig lives there. It shines out over the sea to warn boats about the rocks under the waves."

The sprite's eyes shone. "I always wondered why it did that."

"And the bright colours that flow down the river are from the dyeing pools further upstream. I could take you to see them if you like. If you can go into fresh water." Crimson twisted her sleeve. Maybe that was an insensitive thing to say to a creature that lived in the sea.

"That's amazing. Maybe I'll take you up on that. Not today though, I've got too much to do. Well thank you very much for answering those questions. Will you come back? I have loads more."

"Er…another time maybe. I've got to prepare a wedding for my best friend."

"Is that why everyone was down at the beach today? I thought it was more crowded than usual."

"Sort of. The Great Lobster told everyone about the weather for the harvest."

"Ooo I can forecast weather. Do you want me to show you?"

"Er, no thanks. I've got the weather rock for that." The Saffron Vale weather rock was nothing more than a rock hung on a string, but it was always accurate. If it was wet, you could guarantee it was raining. If it blew this way and that, you knew it was windy. "You couldn't tell me my future though, could you? That is, if it's not too much trouble."

"No, no, that's fine. It's the least I can do after you answered my questions. Come on. I'll write it in the sand." The sprite skipped towards the shore and stepped onto the rough sand. "Now, the first thing you've got to know about the future is that it's changeable. Don't pay it too much heed, people go mad that way." The sprite stopped on the shoreline, picked up a piece of seaweed and stared at it before tossing it back on the ground.

Crimson peered over its shoulder. "Shouldn't you write it a bit further inland, so the sea doesn't wash it away?"

"That's the whole point. The future is transient – trans-sea-ent, get it? It's not fixed. Now, here's a good spot. Come on, you'll want to get a good look before it disappears."

The sprite bent over and began to mark the sand with tiny looping writing. After a while, the foam sprite stood back, put their hands on their hips and gave a nod, satisfied with their work.

You will only get your heart's desire if you loosen your laces.

"What does that mean?" asked Crimson.

"No idea." The sprite shrugged. "I just write what I see."

"Does that mean the wedding will go well?"

Another shrug.

Lief appeared behind Crimson, making her jump again. Even the cat-like felinix didn't move so soundlessly. "What did it say?"

"Something about loosening my laces. It makes no sense."

"I told you people go mad thinking about the future. Best not to worry too much about it. Ooo, that's a nice shell." The sprite's gaze fixed on the smooth pearlescent shell in Lief's hand.

"It's yours."

"Ta, mister. Good luck with the future." The sprite snatched up the shell and dived back into the sea, vanishing into the foamy waves.

"Are you ready to go back now?" Lief asked.

Crimson shivered. Her dress was soaked. Again. She'd give anything for a hot bath, but there wasn't time for that. She had to keep working; there was still so much to do. Sometimes she wished she could slow down and relax, like a normal person, but that would have to wait until after the wedding. So she nodded and headed back towards the town, leaving a trail of seawater as she went.

Chapter 30

~ The Lobster Do ~

TWO WEEKS BEFORE THE wedding, Crimson had learned of a Saffron Vale custom called 'a lobster do'. Some research later – research was a strong word; she'd asked any locals she came across – and she had discovered that it was a send-off for the soon-to-be newlyweds; a celebration of their single lives and an excuse to get drunk with friends. She had also found out that the chief bridesmaid was expected to organise one for the bride.

One week before the wedding and Crimson had arranged for Ayla to meet her at the Salt and Pickle Inn for the bride's lobster do while the men mustered at the Drunken Gull for the maire's equivalent. So now she sat in the booked booth, decorated with bunting in the shape of lobsters, with all the women she could round up, waiting for Ayla to join them.

"Please don't say anything about Ayla's baking."

"I won't." Dilly huffed and took a long drink of beer.

"Just don't ruin her lobster do."

"For the fifth time, I am not going to say anything about her baking. I'm not a total idiot. And why did you invite me if you're so sure I'm going to say something?"

Crimson blinked at the petalborn. "Because you're my friend." One of few people she had got to know well in Saffron Vale, and she couldn't imagine a world where her friends weren't friends. Stitches. Now she had forced Dilly and Ayla into an awkward situation. That sprite had got in her head about loosening up and now she was too loose, and it was all going to go wrong.

"Look, the elf can bake. Her biscuits at the game night were delicious. I've got nothing against her as a person. But if she tries to compete with my brother…Family comes before friends. You understand?"

Crimson swallowed hard. If her mother were alive, maybe she'd agree with Dilly, but Crimson had grown up an orphan and left the people who had raised her for a new life. Her friends were all she had, and they were too precious to lose. "Just…be nice. Everything has to be perfect."

"Stop putting so much pressure on yourself. A lobster do is meant to be messy." Greezi toyed with the teal paper umbrella in her martini glass. "It's a chance to let your hair down, maybe meet some men, have some fun. There's no rules. That's the point."

Crimson frowned. A lobster do sounded like chaos and that wasn't something she usually allowed in her ordered life.

Greezi elbowed her in the ribs. "Relax a bit. You're so stiff I could use you as a board."

"Crimson?" Ayla's voice caught her off-guard.

"Surprise!" everyone yelled, causing the patrons in the inn to jolt up from their pints.

"Oh Crimson, you organised me a lobster do, thank you so much." Ayla pulled Crimson into a hug and accepted a headband with sequinned scarlet lobsters attached to springs that made them bobble around with the slightest movement. "Jojo's been going on about his all week. They're taking over the Drunken Gull and there are all sorts of surprises organised, and he said something about a sheep..."

Crimson's cheek muscles tensed, turning her smile into more of a grimace. What had Lief planned? He hadn't told her anything about the maire's do and now he was going to outshine her. "I thought we'd have a girls' night together. I brought a deck of cards, and we can play games, tell jokes that sort of thing. Who wants to play Pin the Claw on the Lobster?"

"Pshaw. That's a children's game." Greezi slammed her drink down on the table, causing a dribble of her pink cocktail to spill onto the floor. "First, we need cocktails for everyone. Then we can play I Have Never."

"What's I Have Never?" Crimson's brow crinkled. This

wasn't what she'd expected.

"It's very simple. We go round the circle and say what we've never done. If you have done it, you drink. Don't worry, you'll get the hang of it."

"Sounds fun." Ayla leaned forward, her eyes sparkling with excitement.

"Right, barkeep, a pitcher of your most extravagant cocktail and keep 'em coming!"

The cyclops bartender shook his head and mixed up a concoction of spirits and fizz that bubbled pink as he poured it into strange, shaped glasses before handing them out.

"Delicious," Greezi said, licking her lips. "Now, I'll start. I have never woken up in bed with a man."

Crimson dipped her head and took a small sip while the rest of the women hooted with laughter as they either drank or kept their glasses on the table. The cocktail was a dangerous combination of sweet juice with the barest tang of alcohol, easy to drink too much of.

~

"I just need some fresh air." Crimson stumbled outside into the main street and leaned against the cool wall of the inn. She closed her eyes and stifled a yawn. She'd worked too many early mornings and late nights getting everything ready for the wedding, and she felt the lack of sleep down to her bones.

The drink didn't help either. She was the least adventurous of the group and hadn't drunk much, but whatever was in that pale pink cocktail had gone straight to her head and no one else showed any signs of slowing down. The I Have Never game had become increasingly outrageous, and Crimson's mind boggled at the sorts of things people had done.

She'd expected some avantgarde activities from Sibby, the national showperson, but this evening she had got an insight into the maire's bedroom antics that she could have gone a lifetime without knowing and she needed a break.

Pull yourself together, Brouderer. Crimson forced her eyes open. Ruining Ayla's lobster do because she was tired was not an option. Crimson pinched the back of her hands in an effort to wake herself up. When that didn't work, she slipped a hand into her pocket and pricked a finger with a pin. Sucking her finger, Crimson turned to go back inside when she heard a familiar voice.

"I can't believe you made it." What was the maire doing here? Wasn't he meant to be on the other side of town at the Drunken Gull celebrating his own lobster do? "I thought the carriage would never come."

Crimson made to step forward and ask him if everything was alright – Lief was meant to organise the boys' night out, but he was such a loner that he probably made everyone drink in different corners of the pub. Stitches, did she have to do everything? What did men even do at these parties?

She had taken half a step away from the wall when another

figure came into the light. Crimson froze and watched as the new figure – a female figure – moved closer to the maire in a familiar way.

"You have no idea how glad I am to see you." The maire held out his arms, and the female stepped into them.

"I couldn't bear to stay away." The newcomer had a distinct female voice with a Capital City accent. Small antlers crested her head, poking out from between her curly hair. "But the coach threw a wheel in Innton and I got stuck there."

Crimson stopped breathing. She watched with growing horror as their shadowed forms came together, too far from the solitary flickerfire streetlamp for her to make out more than silhouettes.

They stayed in the embrace for several moments. Longer than if they were friends. He didn't pull back. If anything, he leaned into it.

Awful man. Hateful satyr. How could he do this to Ayla? Crimson turned to get her friend. Ayla had to see what the maire was capable of.

The rest of the maire's lobster party appeared, singing a lewd song about a sheep. They cheered when they saw the groom-to-be and surrounded him and his lover.

A couple left the Salt and Pickle Inn and a bubble of laughter wafted behind them from the warmth of the interior. Crimson recognised Ayla's familiar giggle, and a lump formed in her throat. Her friend would be crushed. But better to know. Crimson would want to know. Not that she had a significant other, but…she would want to know, to make an informed decision.

Crimson swallowed and backed into the shadows as the lobster party turned a corner, the maire arm in arm with the newcomer. There was still a chance that this was all a big misunderstanding. Maybe they were close friends or some sort of relation and the maire was innocent, just like Lief had been when Crimson had thought he was with Bircha.

The maire's voice sounded over the street, shouting to be heard over the din from the other men, still singing the same two lines in a never-ending loop. "Come back to my place. The others are already there."

That sealed it. He was cheating on Ayla. On their lobster do night. A week before the wedding. Despicable satyr. He probably couldn't help himself; the stereotype of the horny old goat who loved a party was a stereotype for a reason. Crimson watched them go.

"Come back inside, Crimson, you're missing the party." Ayla leaned out of the inn's door, flooding the grey street with warm firelight.

Crimson turned her face away from where the maire had disappeared with his paramour's arm linked through his. She would have to tell Ayla the truth about her fiancé. Better that she knew now that he was a no-good cheat than after they were married. She took Ayla's hand and led her back inside. If she were going to ruin her best friend's life, at least she could give her the news somewhere warm.

"What's the matter, Crimson? You look like you've seen a ghost."

"Maybe she's seen something else." Sibby waggled their eyebrows suggestively and nudged Bircha in the stomach.

Crimson didn't say anything, her mind still reeling from what she'd seen. Ayla headed straight back to the booth where the women sat drinking and giggling.

"Sit by me and have a drink. And don't worry so much. You're always worrying." Ayla leaned forward and brushed Crimson's hair out of her face. The elf turned serious. "You worry too much, you need to lose control sometimes. Take it from someone older and wiser than you. You need to seize the moment, enjoy yourself and…and…stop planning down to the last detail."

"But–"

"No buts."

"Who said butts?" Sibby asked.

"OK, OK, I've got a game," Greezi said, slamming her glass onto the table. "Who has the best behind in Saffron Vale?"

Ayla cackled and screamed, "My Jojo."

Crimson smiled at her friend. She would tell her, but not now. Not when she was so happy and long past tipsy and on her way to totally smashed. There would be time for hard truths tomorrow. For now, she tried her best to loosen up and play along as the lady lobsters debated the merits of satyr posteriors.

Chapter 31

~ The day after the night before ~

CRIMSON TOOK HER FRIEND'S hands in hers. She had made up an excuse to see Ayla the following day, in the evening, once she was sure her head had stopped throbbing. Those colourful drinks had a lot to answer for they were almost worse than scrumpy. Crimson fought a shudder. Nothing was worse than a scrumpy hangover.

She hadn't wanted Ayla to go home and find the maire in flagrante delico with a faun, so she'd insisted the elf stay over, but Ayla had left in the morning while Crimson was still asleep. Now, they sat back in her shop, Ayla looking anxious. As well she might, Crimson had said something vague about a wedding emergency when she'd posted the handwritten note through the maire's door. She couldn't risk seeing him in person. She wasn't sure what she would do to the person who hurt Ayla.

Crimson took a deep breath and started, "I know this is hard to hear." Ayla's brow crinkled and one delicate wrinkle appeared on her forehead. Crimson swallowed. "And I say this as your friend."

"Best friend." Ayla squeezed her hand.

"Right. So you know I have your best interests at heart."

"Of course. What's going on, Crimson? What's wrong with the wedding?"

Crimson swallowed again, her throat the approximate consistency of sandpaper as she prepared to destroy her friend's happiness. "I saw Maire, I mean Jollivity," Ayla's frown turned to a sappy smile, "with someone in the street…on his lobster do."

"Who?"

"I don't know, but they were close."

"He does have a lot of friends. You've seen the guest list. It's incredible how many people he knows!"

"They were a bit…more than friends."

The crinkle between Ayla's brow came back. "What do you mean?"

Stitches. She would have to spell it out. "There was canoodling."

"Canoodling." Ayla repeated the word as if she could find a hidden depth to it.

"A cuddle."

"I see." Ayla bit her lip. "With whom?"

"A faun, I think. They had antlers. And then I saw them walking back to his house."

"Oh." Ayla trembled under her hands.

"I'm so sorry, Ayla, but I couldn't not tell you, I couldn't risk you starting a life together based on a lie. I could kill him for hurting you, or at least maim him in some way. I'm pretty handy with my fabric scissors. Anyway, I...why are you laughing?"

Ayla's shoulders shook with silent mirth. "Go on, you're in a good flow."

"What have I missed?" Crimson squinted at her friend and let go of Ayla's hands.

"Are you sure you're finished? I liked the bit where you threatened him with your fabric scissors; only a good friend would go that far."

"You're making fun of me, but those scissors are sacred."

"I know. You are a good friend, but you needn't worry, Crimson."

"No?"

"That's just one of Jojo's friends. She stayed overnight, along with about half a dozen others. I had linner with them before I left to come here."

"Oh. Right. Well, that clears that up then." Crimson buried her head in her hands. "I'm such an idiot." Some part of her still couldn't quite believe that Ayla had chosen the maire for her life mate, so she'd thought the worst of him instead of trying to see what her best friend saw in the man she loved.

"No, it's sweet that you care. But I promise you that Jojo isn't like that. He might flirt with the world, but he comes home to me. You've never met a more married man, and we're not even married yet."

"Sorry if I worried you."

"You should take more care of your own love life and stop looking out for everyone else's."

Crimson looked away. That comment hit closer to home than she liked to admit. "I haven't got time to think about a love life."

It was Ayla's turn to lean forward and take Crimson's hands. "Maybe that's a problem."

"Hmphf."

"You always work hard. Ever since we met, you've been busy with one project or another. I understand that you want to please everyone and prove you can do this all by yourself, but I'm worried for you. Take it from someone older and wiser; stop putting off things that can make you happy. If you don't take a risk with Lief then you'll never know if it can go anywhere. I know I'm glad I took the leap with Jojo."

"How did you get to be so wise?"

Ayla sniffed. "It's our long lives that make elves so wise."

"You're not that much older than me, are you?"

"I'm an elf. We live for centuries; automatic wisdom."

Crimson pulled a face. "That's not how it works."

Ayla brushed off her comment with a wave of her elegant hand.

"Alright, o wise one. I have a question for you," Crimson said.

Ayla raised an eyebrow and waited.

"What is linner?"[3]

---

[3] As you may already know, dear reader, linner is a small meal you may take between lunch and dinner. It's similar to brunch only without the breakfast.

Chapter 32

~ *The final checks* ~

CRIMSON STEPPED BACK TO admire her work. Everything was finished. Or as finished as it could be. Ayla would be here any minute for her last night as a single elf and Crimson had set up everything she could think of so her friend would have a relaxing time. A selection of books sat on the kitchen table alongside a takeaway pie from the bakery and cakes from the Cozy Lobster, so neither of them had to worry about cooking.

She had even set up yoghurt, oats and honey so they could recreate teenage days together where they'd made face masks and discussed every trivial thing happening in Oasis. Although Crimson didn't want to hear any more details about the maire or his amorous antics.

Crimson did a final walk around the dresses, plucking off a

stray thread. Sibby's show dress sparkled in yellow and green. Crimson sucked on her lip as she fluffed out the skirt on Ayla's white dress.

She had added gemstones and embroidery in silver thread, so it shimmered delicately as the evening light caught the fabric. The skirt floated and the underskirt had matching embroidery so it wouldn't look plain at the evening party – she hadn't been able to talk her friend out of a reveal dress for the evening.

But was it enough? What would Lief think? His face had come into her thoughts more and more as the wedding approached. Did he still like her? After she'd told him she couldn't be in a relationship with him. And now that the wedding was almost here, she had the horrible feeling that they could have made it work and she'd wasted more time not being with him because she'd put up barriers that didn't need to exist.

"What do you think?" she asked Smudge, partly about the dress and partly because she had spoken to him about her Lief dilemma so often when alone in her shop that he must have opinions on the subject.

The small dragon tilted his head to one side and made a choking noise. Crimson hurried him downstairs and into the small courtyard garden before he sneezed and destroyed her hard work. She left him to sniff around and went back upstairs for one last look.

A glint of silver in the corner of the room caught her eye.

"What do you think, little luck spider? Is it enough?"

Crimson had put her soul into making this dress beautiful for her friend, she had wished Ayla every happiness and good fortune with every careful stitch. She still didn't know if she had magic, but as she sewed, she had felt that same lightness and swirling of colours that she had experienced before and she had willed any luck magic she had into the threads as she plied her craft.

She picked up the latest letter from her teggish friend and re-read it:

Dear Crimson,

I knew you would ask about accessing the aether. Sadly, I cannot tell you how best to do that, I can only try to explain how I do it.

For me, it is as simple and as complicated as unfocusing my mind and letting it wander. Almost like those magical pictures where you can see something underneath when you relax your eyes – have you seen them? I saw one once of a woman – or was it two women? – and if you relaxed your eyes and tilted your head, suddenly it was no longer a woman but a candlestick. It is something similar to that.

And if you do it right, then you can access the aether and all the magic within it.

Crimson had tried to do what Artor had recommended ever

since she'd received the letter, but the closest she'd come was the time she'd experienced the room swirling when thinking of her mother. And the more she thought on it, the more likely it was that she'd been light-headed.

But you do not need magic. Look at everything you've achieved without it. Hard work, focus and, yes, a smidgeon of good luck so you can seize those opportunities are all you need to succeed in your life.

One day, I hope we can meet in person, and I can answer your questions more fully. Until then, I wish you every joy and luck in your new project. The papers have already been speculating about the wedding in your vale. It sounds exciting, and I expect to hear all about it in your next letter.

Wishing you all the best, your friend,

Artor Voeux

She took a deep breath. "Well, I wish Ayla every piece of luck and joy in her marriage."

The spider stilled in its web. Crimson glanced up to see a single *yes* written among the shimmering silky strands.

A good omen, she decided.

A knock at the door announced Ayla's arrival, and Crimson hurried downstairs to greet her friend.

"Good evening, bride-to-be!"

"Good evening, bridesmaid-to-be! Can you believe it? This time tomorrow, I'll be a wedded woman." Happiness shone from Ayla and Crimson smiled.

"I know."

"And it's all thanks to you introducing us."

"You would have found each other in the end."

Ayla considered this. "Perhaps, but all I know is that I owe you a debt…"

"You owe me nothing. Especially not on the day before your wedding!"

"So, you aren't interested in this chocolate mud cake I made?"

"I didn't say that."

Ayla laughed. "Did you make the face masks?"

"Come on, I've got everything ready."

Chapter 33

~ The morning of the wedding ~

CRIMSON AWOKE ON THE morning of the wedding to a clattering in her kitchen. It took her a moment to place it because she wasn't used to hearing the sound of cooking in her house, but that was the unmistakable clang of a pot and / or pan and – she sniffed – the sizzle of bacon filled the room.

Wrapping herself in her patchwork dressing gown made from the remnants of many pieces of cloth she had cut for her clients, she headed downstairs.

"What are you doing? The bride isn't meant to cook breakfast on her wedding day."

Ayla looked up guiltily from her spot near the cast iron stove. "I couldn't sleep. Besides who else was going to cook breakfast? You?"

Crimson grasped at her chest as if Ayla had shot a crossbow bolt there. "Ouch. That hurt. And no, I was going to order breakfast from Greezi's shop."

Ayla dismissed Crimson's idea with a wave of her long hand. "She'll be too busy with the catering. You do know it's the wedding today?"

Crimson bit the inside of her cheek. "I do have some idea. The bride in my kitchen is a bit of a giveaway. How long have you been awake for?" Crimson eyed the stove. It took at least an hour to get to cooking temperature unless her friend had magic that Crimson didn't know about.

She looked around for Smudge.

"I've let your dragon out already." Ayla placed two hot rolls onto mismatched plates she pulled from Crimson's cupboards and laid the perfectly cooked bacon next to it. "Breakfast is served."

"Did you bake these?"

Ayla looked away, avoiding the question. "I can't believe it's today. It's felt like it was ages away forever and now it's here. The big day." She took a nervous bite of her sandwich.

Crimson did some fuzzy early morning mental arithmetic. Bread took time to make; kneading, proving, baking. Her friend must have been up for hours. Crimson slipped into a chair and picked at the roll. She often forgot about breakfast, and she never ate this early.

"Ayla, you don't have to do anything you don't want to do. Everyone will understand if you decide to call it off."

The elf laughed. "Silly Crimson, you know just what to say to cheer me up. As if I'd call off the wedding. I want to marry Jojo, but sometimes…"

Crimson cut the bread with a satisfying crack of the crust and layered her bacon inside it, waiting for Ayla to finish her thought.

"Sometimes I wish it hadn't gotten quite so…big. As the nun said to the priest."

Crimson snorted. "That's the maire talking."

Ayla grinned. "I suppose it is. He's rubbed off on me. As the nun said."

Crimson choked on her sandwich.

Ayla sighed. "Anyway, did you know we have over a thousand guests?"

Crimson nodded. She did know. She'd made the list for the invites, thank you very much, and organised the catering, and given the numbers to Dilly and Duncan for the cake. She knew that there were exactly one thousand three hundred and two people coming to the wedding.

Ayla carried on, oblivious to Crimson's mental cataloguing. "Sometimes I think maybe we should have eloped, had a quiet wedding somewhere and then run away on honeymoon. But Jojo's too dedicated to the vale for anything that dramatic."

Smudge wandered in from his morning ablutions and

snagged a rasher of bacon from an unguarded plate.

"You don't want your family to see you?" Crimson asked between bites.

"I do. It's just that Jojo is such a public figure. People have come from all over the queendom to join in the celebrations and, it's not really me. But I suppose I'll have to get used to the life of celebrity."

Crimson ate some more of her bacon roll. The maire might be a well-known and respected – or tolerated – figure in Saffron Vale and he knew a lot of people across the queendom, but she wouldn't have said he was a celebrity.

"It makes it difficult to know where to go on honeymoon. We want to relax and enjoy ourselves but, with Jojo being so noticeable, it's hard to pick somewhere."

"You could ask him to stop wearing those waistcoats. Then he'd blend right in."

"You are funny, Crimson." Ayla wiped a tear from her eye.

Crimson finished her roll. She hadn't been joking. She'd seen what the maire had chosen for his wedding outfit. His gold waistcoat could outshine the sun.

"What time is Sibby getting here?"

Crimson looked out of the window at the first fingers of dawn cresting across the sky like dusky pink ribbons unfurling on grey satin. "Not until sunrise, at least. What do you want to do until they arrive?"

"Can I see the dress one more time?"

Crimson smiled and followed Ayla back upstairs, where the dress stood on its mannequin by the window.

"Crimson, you are clever." Ayla pulled her into a hug. "I don't know how you've done it, but it's even better than the last time I saw it." A tear fell down her face.

Crimson blinked at the dress. Overnight it had transformed. Glittering thin silks hung over it in a web design that highlighted the delicate fabric and intricate embroidery. She reached out to touch the gossamer thin coating…almost like a spider web.

She glanced up to the corner of the room where a small, silver luck spider now hung in its web. The words *you're welcome* shone in its threads.

"Thank you," she mouthed at the spider. The spider did nothing to indicate that it acknowledged her, but Crimson took reassurance from the fact that it was there.

Chapter 34

~ *Getting ready* ~

S IBBY ARRIVED AN HOUR after dawn, carrying a large wooden box with reinforced hinges that they carried with ease, the muscles on their biceps bulging under their rosetted fur. "Darrlings, I have arrived."

Even this early in the morning, Sibby wore a full face of makeup complete with false eyelashes and special paint on their fur to bring out their cheekbones.

"Hurry up." Crimson drew her dressing gown tight over her pyjamas, conscious that she looked a mess as she ushered Sibby into the kitchen where Ayla was on her fifth cup of coffee. The elf now vibrated as she sat trying to read an old issue of The Golden Acorn newspaper.

"Tsk, tsk. We can't have you like this on your wedding day," Sibby said as she prowled around the elf. "I need you to relax if I'm going to make you look even more beautiful than you already are."

Ayla giggled.

"Do you have any wine?" Sibby asked.

Crimson shook her head. After her scrumpy hangover, she saved alcohol for special occasions and didn't keep any in the house.

"A pity, but never mind, I always come prepared." Sibby dug around in their box and pulled out a green bottle. They twisted the cork out with a satisfying pop. "We need glasses, darrling."

Crimson found three clean glasses in the cupboard and placed them on the table where Sibby gave them a onceover with a critical eye.

"Not the right type for wine, but I suppose they'll do. Drink this," they handed a glass to Ayla, "it will counteract the coffee. Once you've stopped shaking, I can start my masterpiece."

It didn't take long for Ayla to calm down and while they waited, Sibby laid out brushes and palettes of paint and powder in every shade of the rainbow. Crimson picked up a set to study the shimmer on a palette of greens that ranged from sage all the way through to dark pine forests. If only fabric could take the colours as easily as Sibby could paint them on.

"Now, I assume you want to go for something natural,

darrling? When you've got such a perfect canvas to start with, you don't want to overpaint it. Unless you want to be bold?"

Crimson eyed Sibby's dark eyeshadow that made her feline eyes look huge with a combination of allure mixed with danger that spoke of late nights and smoky bars. The felinix was used to performing at shows with low lighting and had a flair for the dramatic…Crimson began to question the wisdom of having the performer do Ayla's hair and makeup for her wedding.

Crimson moved a palette of yellows away from Ayla's questing fingers. "I think your fiancé loves you for who you are, so we just want to enhance that."

Ayla beamed. "You're right, of course, Crimson. Let's save the bold colours for another day. You can teach me how to apply them."

"Of course. And don't worry, darrling, I'll get to you in a moment."

"Oh yes, you must do Crimson too." Ayla nodded in agreement, almost spilling her drink over Smudge, who still circled the table in search of stray pieces of bacon.

"There's really no need…"

"Don't worry, you're in safe hands. We need to have you looking gorgeous in case there's a lovely man at the wedding you want to snog."

Crimson choked on her water and went to check on the dress, in case it had moved in the last ten minutes. Dresses could be tricky like that.

Once Crimson had reassured herself that the wedding dress was fine, and her own outfit was ready, and Sibby's ensemble hadn't dissolved into a mess overnight, she went back downstairs.

She needn't have worried. Sibby had used makeup to enhance Ayla's features, making her glow with a radiance that would make sure all eyes were on her. The felinix was in the middle of pinning up Ayla's hair into a complicated up do with a single lustrous blonde lock curling down over her neck.

"Ayla, you look gorgeous."

Ayla beamed at Crimson. "Do you think so?" Crimson nodded in response to the unnecessary question. Ayla would have looked gorgeous smeared in mud with leaves in her hair; this morning she looked ethereal. "Do you think Jojo will like it?"

"Of course. Besides, if he loves you, shouldn't he love you no matter what you look like?"

Ayla's gaze took on that mooning wistfulness that she got whenever she thought about the maire.

Sibby hissed out a breath and paused in weaving the dried crocus petals through Ayla's hair. "If he can still take a breath when he sees you for the first time today, I haven't done my job properly. There. Go look in the mirror and bask in my masterpiece."

Ayla skipped off to the front of the shop, where Crimson

had a full-length mirror. A squeal of delight had Sibby smiling. "Now, darrling, it's your turn. Sit."

"There's no need." Crimson held up her hands as if that could fend off the makeup brush that Sibby waved.

"Nonsense. You're part of the wedding party. I cannot let you stand next to Ayla with a," they shuddered, "bare face."

Crimson's fingers traced her cheeks. "Is it really that bad?"

"Hmmm? No, darrling, don't be silly. You're gorgeous. But, thanks to my skills, Ayla now looks divine. Trust me, a little highlight here and colour there and you'll be able to hold your head high next to her, and don't worry, I'll make sure you won't outshine her." Sibby tapped a manicured claw to her jaw. "Now, what colour shall we use on your eyes? They're so unusual…"

Crimson screwed her rainbow-flecked eyes closed. Of course she would be a problem.

"Green," said Ayla, reappearing in the kitchen doorway. "It goes best with her hair."

"Grreen," Sibby repeated. "Yes. Now sit still."

Crimson sat on her hands while Sibby worked her magic and Ayla sipped more wine.

~

Crimson stared at her reflection. The woman in the mirror looked like a more attractive version of her, like someone who hadn't spent months worrying about a wedding, like someone who knew how to have fun. She reached up a hand to pat her hair.

Sibby knocked her fingers away with the metallic comb.

"Ouch!" Crimson rubbed the back of her hand.

"Don't touch! You'll ruin all my hard work." Sibby used their comb to punctuate their point. "Now, do you two need any help getting dressed?"

Crimson shook her head, shaking out her hurting hand. There would be a bruise, she was sure.

"Then I'll go. Perfection takes a while you know, darrlings. Do you have my costume for tonight?"

Crimson nodded and led the way upstairs. Sibby circled the mannequin and pronounced themselves happy. "Perfect. But how can I take it to my room?"

"I have a bag." Crimson retrieved a clothes bag from under her bed and laid it over the blankets before turning to unfasten the yellow and green dress from its mannequin. She pointed out the reveal trick to Sibby as she went.

"Yes, yes, you told me all that last time. But how did you do this on the wedding dress?"

"I had a little luck." Crimson mouthed another thank you at the luck spider, which stayed still in its web.

Sibby reached out a clawed hand to touch the wedding dress. Crimson leapt across the room and whacked her hand out of the way with a coat hanger.

"Ouch." Sibby licked the back of their hand with a rough tongue.

"Don't touch! You'll ruin all my hard work," Crimson repeated Sibby's words back to them.

"Touché."

Crimson finished with the dress, struggling to carry the weighted fabric the short distance to her bed. Once she made it, she laid it in the linen bag and fastened the toggles on the bag, hiding it away from any dust or mud Sibby might encounter on the way back to their suite.

"Thank you, darrling. Now I must away and prepare. I'll see you at the wedding." With that, Sibby hoisted the dress over one shoulder as if it weighed nothing and sauntered downstairs with a practiced sway of their hips.

"Do you think I should walk down the aisle like that?" Ayla mused, watching Sibby leave.

"I think if you tried that in your wedding gown, you'd take out half the guests."

Ayla laughed and eyed the cloud-white dress. "So, how do I get this on?"

Crimson took the wineglass from Ayla's hand and told her to wait as she disrobed the mannequin, holding her breath in case the silvery webs came off in her fingers. They didn't and Crimson motioned for her friend to take off her fluffy towelled dressing gown as she held the dress out for Ayla to step into.

Once Ayla's long legs were in the skirt, Crimson lifted the dress until it sat in place before moving round to the back to fasten the hooks, eyes and buttons that would keep the gown in place.

"Crimson, you've given me curves!"

"I just accentuated what was already there." Crimson allowed herself a smile as she double checked the fastenings. The last thing anyone wanted was the bride's dress to fall down in the middle of the ceremony. She looked Ayla up and down and gasped. The hem. It dragged on the floor. Stitches! How could she make such a stupid mistake? There wasn't time to rehem the entire skirt; it required removing the lace frill at the bottom, turning up the inner layer and then restitching the lace on with invisible stitches, not to mention it would ruin the spider web effect.

"Oh Ayla, I'm so sorry…"

"Hmmm? What about?" Ayla asked as she slipped her feet into her heeled shoes and the dress lifted to skim the floor. She gave a dainty twirl, feeling the balance of the dress.

"Oh, nothing, just a loose thread." Crimson picked off the imaginary thread and shook her head. Shoes. She had made the length to fit her friend in her shoes. Of course. She could breathe again.

"I feel like a princess."

Crimson smiled.

"I'm serious. I bet the queen doesn't have a gown this

beautiful. And, what's this?" Ayla's hands had traced her curves and found slits in the skirt. "You gave me pockets? Brilliant! And the skirt comes off, right?"

"Yes. When you want to change, just unclip here, lift and pull. I can help you with it later. Not now! If you take it off, it'll take too long to hook it back on." Crimson pulled Ayla's hands away from the hidden fastenings that would allow her to remove the skirt.

"You'd better get ready too, unless you're planning to go in your dressing gown."

Crimson looked down at her patchwork robe and gave a twirl. "I think it could start a new trend."

Ayla laughed, kicked off her shoes, and went searching for her wine as Crimson slipped into her dress; a dandelion stem green confection with a tight bodice and full skirt that matched the underskirt for Ayla's reveal dress and didn't clash with the yellows and purples that made up the rest of the colour scheme. She slipped her travel sewing kit into one of the concealed pockets and ran her fingers over her sides to make sure there was no bulky shape to ruin the silhouette.

They went downstairs with exaggerated care, lifting their long skirts so they didn't trip and bending their necks so they couldn't mess up their hair dos by accidentally knocking into the ceiling. Admittedly, that was more of a problem for Ayla than for Crimson and, for once, she didn't resent her teg heritage.

Ayla strode to the front of the shop and hovered by the

window, alternating between smoothing her dress and picking at her shaped nails.

Crimson put their shoes by the counter and fussed over the bouquets, making sure everything was ready. She mumbled the running order of the day under her breath and counted off on her fingers everything that still needed to happen. She ran out of fingers quickly.

A flash of movement caught her eye, and Crimson whipped round, her skirt fanning out around her legs. She paused as she realised the movement was her own reflection in the mirror. Crimson stepped closer. Her reddish hair, normally tucked into a neat braid, was in a complicated crown plait that lent a few much-needed inches to her small height. And her face had never looked so clear or radiant. She was nothing compared to her elvish friend, of course, but she might actually be…attractive. It was a strange thought, something to dwell on later.

Crimson was so focused on her work and building her business, that she'd never actually thought too much about how she looked except that she had to look neat and competent – her appearance was an extension of her ability as a dressmaker. Guilder Senda had taught her that.

Of course, it was far too much makeup for everyday wear, and she wouldn't know how to recreate the smudgy emerald eyeshadow that highlighted her eyes and gave her a sultry sophistication she certainly never usually possessed. She blushed as she wondered what a certain warden might say when he saw her.

A squeal from Ayla interrupted Crimson's study of her reflection, and she turned her back on the mirror to see what had excited her friend.

"The transport's here," Ayla said from her spot at the window before yanking open the door, ignoring Crimson's pleas to put her shoes on.

Crimson grabbed the bouquets and Ayla's delicate slippers and raced out, squatting to slip them onto Ayla's feet. It didn't matter if her own dress got ruined. She repeated the phrase as she brushed off a speck of dirt and lifted Ayla's skirts, so they didn't brush the ground.

Crimson looked up and her heart sank. One of the maire's curvy carts waited outside her shop.

Chapter 35

~ *The Wedding* ~

CRIMSON CLIMBED INTO THE curvy cart with no small amount of trepidation. Her last journey in the vehicle had been…bumpy, and that was a generous description.

"Are you sure this is how you want to arrive at your wedding? There's still time to get a horse…"

"Don't be silly, Crimson. It'll be fine. I trust Jojo and besides, this is his pride and joy. How could I say no when he offered it to me?"

Very easily, thought Crimson. But she said, "Very well then, but could we at least move to the front cart? It moves around less and I don't want to throw up on your dress. Not after I spent so long on it."

"Silly Crimson. The back is the best place to sit, you get the full curvy cart experience."

"That's what I'm afraid of," Crimson muttered as she joined Ayla on the farthest bench from the front. Smudge curled up under a bench. The small dragon hadn't had the dubious pleasure of riding in one of the carts before and was unencumbered by the fear that seized Crimson's stomach and made her limbs tight.

She distracted herself by arranging Ayla's skirt so her best friend could sit, hoping that the cobwebs wouldn't come off on the cart's seats and then gripped the bench so hard her knuckles turned white in anticipation of the jarring movements.

She wasn't disappointed. The double cart set off alright, but as soon as it turned a corner, the back cart careened out. At their feet, Smudge slipped and slid to the other side of the cart.

Ayla screamed.

Crimson turned to tell her to hold tight before realising the elf was screaming with excitement. In contrast to Crimson, Ayla waved her hands above her head, enjoying the ride.

"That was thrilling," Ayla breathed as they climbed down from the cart.

"That's one word for it." Crimson leaned against the cart, allowing her vision to stop swimming and her feet to get used to the feel of solid ground. If she was alone, she might have crouched down and kissed the dirt. *At least she wouldn't have to get back into the cart on the way back.* Comforting herself with that thought, she tried to focus on the wedding.

Lief met them at the top of the path that led down to the beach. Luckily, it was too narrow for a cart, so they'd have to walk the rest of the way to the ceremony.

Lief stood a little straighter as they approached, his gaze fixed on Crimson as she stepped forward. Having purpose helped to ground her and sped up her recovery from the traumatic journey. "Smudge needs to go first. Have you got the rings?"

Lief leaned in and whispered, "You look gorgeous."

Crimson blushed. Lief's lips quirked in a knowing smile as he knelt next to the small dragon, offering him a fish to keep him busy while he tied the rings into Smudge's bow with dextrous fingers. To stop herself daydreaming over the handsome man kneeling in front of her, Crimson turned to Ayla and fussed with her wedding gown.

By some miracle or luck spider magic, the webs had stayed in place over the fabric, lending a pearlescent shimmer to the tiny gems Crimson had embroidered over the bodice. It had transformed the dress from an elegant gown into a masterpiece that assured Ayla would be centre of attention even when Sibby showed up for the evening's entertainment.

Crimson squinted across the beach. The guests were in place, sitting on chairs that every member of Saffron Vale had contributed to their maire's wedding and even the Great Lobster had turned up to oversee the event. They sat on the shoreline, half in and half out of the water, with the surf lapping at their shell.

At the end of the carpet – bright yellow, naturally – the maire stood next to Hardy, glinting in his gold waistcoat. He kept twisting back to look down the makeshift aisle. It was sweet really, how much he loved her friend. Just as long as he didn't do anything to hurt her. Crimson's eyes narrowed and her fingers went to her emergency sewing kit hidden in a concealed pocket. She could do some damage with her pins and needles if he dared to make Ayla cry.

"Hello? Red?" Lief tapped her shoulder. "You look like you're ready to hurt someone."

"Crimson? Is everything alright?" Ayla regarded her with anxious eyes.

Crimson shook herself. "All good." She offered her arm to Lief. "Ayla, wait until we're at the front with the maire before you start walking down. Slow steps, show off your train. Where's your bouquet?"

Lief raced back to the curvy cart and retrieved the flowers, which he handed to Ayla with great care so he didn't squash the delicate blooms.

"I know how to walk, Crimson."

"OK, OK. Release Smudge."

Lief signalled to Hardy and the clerk pulled something out of his pocket. The purple dragon raced down the aisle without turning aside to sniff any of the interesting things one might find at the seaside, not to mention any of the guests.

"Impressive," Crimson said as her gaze tracked her dragon down the aisle. "How did you do that?"

"Smoked kippers."

"Clever."

"Was that a compliment?" Lief asked, quirking his eyebrow with a tinge of humour.

Crimson opened her mouth, but Ayla cut her off. "When do you think you two will stop flirting and begin walking down the aisle? Because I'd very much like to marry my fiancé today, if you don't mind."

Ayla's nerves must be showing because she'd never be so abrupt normally.

"Sorry." Crimson patted her hand. "Remember, wait until we get to the end, or you won't get the full effect."

Ayla waved them away and focused on her breathing. "In…two…three…Out…two…three."

"Come on." Crimson started forward and Lief kept pace at her side. His arm was stiff and unyielding against hers and she risked a glance at him.

"You're walking like one of those long-legged birds on the water," Crimson said out of the corner of her mouth, a smile fixed on her face as they processed along the yellow carpet.

"A curlew? Or a flamingo?"

Of course, he'd know all the bird names. Know-it-all

warden. "Loosen up. This is a wedding not a walk to your trial."

"Everyone's looking at us."

"That's the point." She glanced at him again. His skin had paled to an unnatural colour under his stubble and his lips were dry. She looked away from his mouth. "It's just the beach. You've walked along here hundreds of times before. Stop overthinking it."

"Easy for you to say. This is probably the sort of thing you do every day."

Crimson rolled her eyes discreetly at his asinine comment, still keeping her smile plastered on her face. She would not ruin the celebration of Ayla's wedding with a sour face. Besides, it was cute. Lief, who she normally thought of as strong and able to take on anything, was a quivering wreck in front of a crowd.

"We're nearly there. Think of how good it will feel when we stop walking."

"It won't feel good..." Lief took a breath in and looked down at her with a strange intensity that made Crimson feel like the nervous one. "It won't feel good because I won't be at your side anymore."

Crimson's mouth fell open. She hadn't expected that. And then they were at the end of the carpet, and she remembered she needed to look happy for her best friend instead of shocked and confused. Her lips curved into her shopkeeper's smile, and she stepped away from Lief's warm body to stand on the left, behind the spot reserved for Ayla.

"Just think, if she doesn't come, the tradition is for the groom to marry the bridesmaid." The maire's comment was strained. Crimson's stomach fell before she realised Maire Bowan was joking. He glanced up the aisle. No Ayla.

He must really love her, Crimson decided as she watched him wring his hands together, then pull at his curly beard, then wring his hands some more.

She angled herself so she could see down the aisle. Where was Ayla? Maybe her friend had changed her mind and seen sense about the small satyr. But Crimson didn't think so. Once Ayla set her mind to something, it happened. Ayla had been the driving force behind moving the family bakery to a better location opposite the Moonlit Mug Café in Oasis, and she'd diversified the business into decorative cakes and biscuits as well as the crusty loaves of bread they were famed for.

But what was taking so long? Maybe she should check. What if there had been a dress malfunction? Or what if Ayla had suddenly been taken ill?

Crimson gathered up her skirts, preparing to dash down the aisle, when Ayla appeared at the end of the yellow carpet.

Chapter 36

~ *The Ceremony* ~

A PLEASING SUSURRATION OF gasps went up from the assembled guests as Ayla began her slow walk down the aisle. Crimson allowed herself a moment to appreciate her work on display. The dress gave Ayla an ethereal beauty that made her seem like some celestial being deigning to visit this plane. Now she was in her heeled slippers, the hem floated at the exact right length to give the illusion that Ayla floated down the aisle. Wisps of her hair caught in the foamy breeze, making her look like a sea nymph on a visit from the ocean depths.

Crimson could almost see her counting out the steps, forcing herself to keep calm as her gaze focused on the satyr standing at the end of the carpet.

"And go petals," Crimson murmured under her breath,

searching out Ovelia and Hamlet, who she had prompted to hand wicker baskets of dried crocus petals out to the guests nearest the aisle. Flutters of purple petals floated in front of Ayla as she walked, contrasting pleasantly with the carpet.

Once all this was done, Crimson would make a Saffron Vale collection, all in bright yellows and purples to echo the crocus that gave the vale its name. Perhaps with red accents to represent their devotion to the Great Lobster, who burbled happy bubbles as Ayla approached.

The elf couldn't keep her steps measured as she got within ten feet of her husband-to-be and she rushed the final paces to the front, her skirt swishing around her and the small jewels sewn to her bodice glinting in the late morning light under the shimmering spider web silk.

Maire Bowan's gaze stayed riveted on his fiancée as she approached, looking as if he might devour her there and then. He stepped towards her and took her hands in his, pulling her in for a kiss in front of everyone.

Crimson blushed on their behalf and looked away, unable to watch her friend's display of affection.

Hardy coughed. Even the town clerk, more used to the maire's customs than most, looked embarrassed. That is to say that his mouth had turned down at the corners in what might have been disapproval, and his paper yellow cheeks had a moue of colour in the centres. Three more ever deliberate coughs later, and Ayla and the maire finally disentangled themselves from one another and took their places in front of the officiant.

"We are gathered here today to celebrate the wedding of Jollivity Bowan and Ayla Sourcrust. If anyone knows of any reason why these two people should not be wed, let them speak now or forever remain silent."

There was a tense pause. Crimson held her breath as she scanned the crowd of guests. For all that she thought that her friend could do better than the chubby satyr, she wanted Ayla to be happy and if someone stood up and said they were already married to the maire, she would…her hands closed on the small snips in her travel sewing kit.

"Well then, let us continue," said Hardy, clapping his hands together. "I believe you have prepared some vows."

"Ayay – Ayla – you have saved this old goat from his bachelor ways. I thought I knew everything there was to know about life and love, that it wasn't for me, that I was doomed to dance alone. But since I met you, I have learned that everything is better with two people[4] and you have opened my eyes to the joy of monogamy. I love you, Ayla Sourcrust, and I want to spend the rest of my days catering to your every whim, fulfilling your every wish. I want to spend the rest of

---

[4] That's not strictly true. There are some things that are infinitely better on your own – reading a book, for example, is an activity best undertaken without other people craning over your shoulder or trying to speak with you. No, I don't want tea. Yes, I am reading. Yes, it is good. Yes, I do want to be left alone. I don't know what the ruddy book is about because every time I try to read it, you interrupt me. Sorry…got a bit carried away there.

my worthless life with you, if you'll take me."

Ayla took a deep breath and grinned down at the maire. "Jollivity Bowan, of course I'll take you. I would take you in any corner of the queendom. I would follow you anywhere you choose to go. Elves live a long time; we see a lot and we know the value of things like friendship and love. It was a friend who introduced us, it was friendship and laughter that brought us together. I feel blessed to say that I have fallen in love with a dear friend, and I look forward to spending the rest of our days together."

They stepped towards each other and clasped hands to the cheers of the guests interspersed with a few wolf whistles.

Hardy coughed before their lips touched. "There are rings to exchange."

The maire shot his clerk a look.

"Who has the rings?" Hardy asked.

Crimson looked round for Smudge. Where was he? Her heart stuttered before she saw him behind Lief. *Oh no, what was he rolling in?*

Crinkling his nose, Lief retrieved the rings and handed them to Hardy. The clerk offered them to the couple. Ayla placed the larger ring on the maire's finger before Maire Bowan did the same, keeping hold of her slender hand and pulling her towards him. Ayla giggled.

Hardy coughed again. "A few signatures to make it legally binding." His lips quirked up at the corners. "If you'll sign here." Hardy pointed to an official-looking parchment laid out on a table brought to the beach for the purpose. A slate grey rock sat in each corner, holding it down. The maire took Hardy's quill and signed, followed by Ayla. "And here." Another signature. "And here." And so it went on.

By the final signature, the maire barely looked at the parchment; instead he gazed at Ayla as if he wanted to gobble her up and his mark was an illegible scrawl. "By the gods Hardy, aren't we married yet?"

The clerk coughed and studied the paperwork for a long moment. He nodded. "I now pronounce you married by the laws of Saffron Vale and the Queendom of Cozy Vales. You may kiss the…" Hardy trailed off. The maire had already yanked Ayla down and claimed her lips with an urgency that was quite unseemly in front of so many people.

By the time they pulled apart, the second chorus of cheers had dissolved into uncomfortable coughs and shuffling of feet.

The maire raised their joined hands above his head and his voice boomed over the beach. "To the afterparty!"

Ayla bent down and whispered in his ear.

"Pictures first, then the afterparty. Right, you lot, get into groups so the sketch artists can do their thing. Hah, Fandangle you old weasel, I'd say make sure they get your good side, but you haven't got one!" the maire brayed out with a laugh.

Crimson stayed where she was as the guests milled about in groups. The sketch artists moved among them, capturing likenesses with swift strokes of their charcoal pencils. Good. It was all good.

She looked up to see Lief still standing opposite her at the end of the carpet. She gave him a nervous smile. He smiled back and started walking towards her.

Maybe this was the time to talk about whatever this thing was that they had or didn't have. Crimson had wanted to put any potential relationship on pause for the wedding, but the truth was that she had been lonely and Lief hadn't been far from her thoughts as she worked on making dresses or arranging seating charts.

This was it; the moment to make her feelings known.

And, as her terrible timing would have it, that was the moment when the maire called his best man over for some sketches and Lief stalked off into the crowd. Crimson took some comfort from the murderous look Lief shot at Maire Bowan before he smoothed his face into something resembling a smile for the sketches.

Later. She would talk to Lief later.

Chapter 37

~ *The Afterparty* ~

"**N**ICE DRESS. BLUE REALLY suits her," Lief said as he sidled up beside Crimson.

"Blue? It's white," Crimson replied, her gaze on the bride.

Lief squinted at Ayla's wedding dress. "Are you sure?"

"Positive. Although…Ig did use some sort of blue to make it brighter." Crimson frowned. "But he promised me it was outside the visible spectrum to most species. Stitches, do you think everyone sees it's blue?"

"Either way, it's gorgeous."

"Yes, but it's supposed to be white like a dandelion clock."

"Oh."

Crimson buried her head in her hands.

"Stop fretting. Ayla's happy. Maire Bowan's happy. That's all that matters, right?"

"You're right. I just wish everyone could see the dress the way it's meant to be."

"Say that again."

"I just wish–"

"Not that."

"Then what?"

"The part where you said I was right."

Crimson swatted Lief's arm, but she couldn't help the small grin that tugged on the corner of her lips. He led her to her seat at the far end of the top table and released her hand with a squeeze. Crimson watched him walk to his own place with a flutter of her heart.

Now that she had finished organising the wedding and sewing the gowns, she would have time in her life for more than work, and that both thrilled and scared her in equal measure. She'd never had such control over her future, never truly had to choose to start a relationship.

What if it all went wrong? What if Lief's feelings had changed? It had been long months of toil and focus to meet her friends' expectations and she wouldn't blame him if he'd decided that she wasn't worth the wait.

Crimson twisted her crisp linen napkin into a messy knot, glancing over at Lief and looking away every time he met her eyes.

Maybe teg magic could help…if she had any. She started to wish before pulling herself out of it. Magic didn't solve things. Wishing wouldn't make anything happen. Working hard and seizing the day was the way forward. She stood. She had to talk to Lief.

Hardy walked to the centre of the room, acting as master of ceremonies as well as the celebrant. The wedding guests stilled, humming with expectation. "Dinner is served."

Crimson sat back down. She would seize the day after enjoying the delicious food.

A rustle of napkins unfurling, and cutlery shuffling chinked through the marquee as the hired servers began to bring out dishes on plain white plates.

Crimson smiled her thanks at the young man who brought her a plate of asparagus with a rich creamy sauce on the side.

"Asparagus with bacon and saffron sauce," he murmured before moving away to serve someone else.

Crimson took a bite and sighed with pleasure as the unctuous sauce mixed perfectly with the crisp asparagus and smoky bacon bits. It was like a dance of flavours in her mouth. Greezi and Pollonius had made something delicious and unique and, oh Artisan, she needed the recipe for this. Crimson tapped her fork on her plate. She didn't cook. Alright, she needed this served somewhere in Woolton because it was perfect.

~

"And now, the cake," announced Hardy.

"You'll want this for the paper." The maire clapped the sketch artist on the shoulder as he strode up to the towering cake.

Dilly and Duncan had outdone themselves. The cake was thirteen tiers high, and the top layers wobbled as the two petalborns wheeled it in on a double cart. Crimson shook her head. She had told them that a curvy cart wasn't appropriate transport for a delicate cake, but the maire had been delighted at the suggestion and so a miniature curvy cart it was.

Delicate crocuses – crocii? She still didn't know – cascaded down the side of the cake in a waterfall of purples with fragile iced stamen glazed in bright saffron yellow peeking out from between the petals.

The maire climbed onto a stepladder so he could match Ayla's height and brandished the ceremonial sword that lay in the back cart. Crimson winced. The blade had come close to Ayla's hair, but the elf trusted her new husband and didn't even flinch as Maire Bowan waved the sword before laying it on the seventh layer of cake; the only one he could reach without stretching. Ayla clasped his chubby hands in her larger ones and together they plunged the sword into the cake and cut a piece.

The maire handed it to Ayla before cutting his own. A

mischievous glint came into Ayla's eyes and her mouth twitched a moment before she crammed her slice into the maire's mouth. He laughed, wiped some icing off his beard and returning the favour, covering Ayla's mouth and chin with sticky icing.

They both dissolved into giggles as Hardy handed them serviettes to wipe away the mess. The maire waved to the assembled guests. "And now for some dancing!"

He gestured to the band sat in the corner of the room and the music changed from gentle background strumming that was barely noticeable to an upbeat folk tune that people could dance to.

The maire led Ayla to the dancefloor, untucked his shirt and twirled around her, stamping his feet with joy as she raised her arms to the air and swayed with an effortless grace, tipping her head back and giving herself to the music. His satyr magic swirled out from the dancefloor, and soon everyone tapped their feet, and guests began to join the couple on the wooden floor.

Crimson didn't trust herself with the maire's joyful magic influencing her. She might do something stupid, like throw herself at Lief. And she needed all her faculties to have the conversation with him.

She moved away from the top table to join Ig at one of the smaller, crowded circular tables at the back of the marquee until the maire's magic caused only the mildest tapping of her toes.

The marquee was thick with joy and celebration, and she couldn't help the smile that sat on her face. Her eyes searched out Lief across the marquee. There was a tension between them that she couldn't place, not the same as the anxiety she'd felt in the run up to the wedding, more a pleasing sort of anticipation as if the barriers she had created had fallen away.

Lief prowled towards her and held out his hand. "Do you want to dance?"

She opened her mouth to say 'yes' when Pollonius appeared at their table.

"Did you like the menu?" Pollonius' chest puffed out with pride, but anxiety or perhaps an eagerness to please lingered in his eyes.

"Of course they did. Didn't you?" asked Greezi, hovering next to him.

Dancing would have to wait. She shot Lief an apologetic smile before replying, "It was delicious. Where did you get your ideas from?"

"Actually, Ig gave us the notion for the main course."

"I did?" Ig hooted with a mix of pleasure and confusion.

"Yes. You said you'd always dreamed of eggs and ham together, so we added a sauce to make it special for the wedding and the muffin underneath."

"Don't forget the sprig of parsley."

Greezi rolled her eyes at Pollonius. "But Eggs Ignatius sounded a bit to heavy on the 'g's—"

"And Eggs Copplebottom wasn't a goer—"

"So we settled on Eggs Benedict."

"Hope you don't mind, Ig?" Pollonius fixed the tylluan with an anxious stare.

Ig's beaky mouth opened into a grin. "I'm honoured—" He looked like he might say more but Milus walked over and, after several stuttering false starts, asked if he wanted to dance while looking at the tylluan askance.

Ig's mouth opened and closed. He pulled out his notebook. The minotaur shoved his hands in his pockets.

Crimson put her hand over Ig's and lowered the notebook out of his eyeline. "It's traditional to dance at weddings, especially with the person who invited you."

"It is?" A glimmer of hope shone in Ig's eyes. Crimson nodded. Ig looked up at Milus who waited, looking all around the room at everything except the tylluan he had just asked for a dance. "Then, yes, I would very much enjoy a dance with you."

Milus grinned from ear to ear and swept Ig away to the dance floor before the tylluan could change his mind.

"Ah, young love," Pollonius gazed after them with a tinge of wistfulness. "I don't suppose you would care for a turn about the dance floor, Greezi?"

"I'd rather cut off my own tusks…but I suppose we could have one dance together." She held up a finger. "Just one, mind you. For the sake of our children."

"Yes, let us strengthen our newfound peace and catering business with a waltz."

"I would never open a catering business with you, you stupid dwarf. Your saffron ratio in the sauce took up almost all of our profits…" The two sauntered off to the dance floor where Hamlet and Ovelia already swayed in time with the music.

Crimson turned to Lief and took a sip of fizzy cider to strengthen her resolve. Just as she had composed the first sentence in her mind, someone whisked him away on urgent best man business and Crimson was left tapping her feet against her chair. Alone again.

She might almost believe it were destiny. That she had her chance at something more, but she had messed it all up by refusing Lief after he had planned a romantic picnic by the rainbow river. Her lips curved up as she remembered the vibrant colours flowing through the water like magic. Maybe that's all it could ever be.

After all, before Lief, the man she'd trusted most in this world had betrayed her to further his own career. Maybe her need for control meant that she couldn't have more than friendship and she should resign herself to that now before she got hurt again.

But if that was the case, then why did her heart skip a beat any time Lief was near? Why did she yearn for evenings snuggled together in his cabin watching the fire crackle and maybe playing a game of cards? And why did she want to press her lips to his and discover if the reality lived up to the memory of their shared kiss back in Innton?

Crimson drank more cider to strengthen her resolve. She had to try. *Tonight,* she vowed to herself, *tonight I will talk to him and give him the chance to decide if he wants to try a relationship or not.* And if he chooses not, then she'd have her answer about whether she should lock up her heart for good.

~

"Copper for your thoughts."

Crimson blinked up at Ayla and accepted the piece of cake she offered with a smile. "Shouldn't you be dancing?"

"In a moment. Being married to a satyr is exhausting."

"You've only been married for about an hour."

"Exactly. He's a party animal."

Crimson turned to the dancefloor where Maire Bowan clomped his hooved feet in a fast rhythm, stirring everyone around him to join in a frenzied dance. She could feel his magic from here; a compulsion to dance, to join in the fun and be merry. Crimson's feet tapped in time with the beat, but she resisted getting up from her seat for now and instead popped one of the decorative chocolate lobsters in her mouth.

The rich chocolate shell dissolved into a smooth salted caramel centre that made her sigh with pleasure before it too faded on her tongue, leaving only the lingering memory of sweet umami flavours.

"Do you like it?" Dilly asked, coming to sit next to them.

"I love it! This is your best chocolate yet."

The petalborn's lips curved into a satisfied smile. "It is, isn't it?"

"This is amazing!" said Ayla. "You should speak to my dad; he'd love to stock these in his bakery, and you'd get queendom-wide acclaim. Dad! Dad! Over here!"

Once Ayla had explained her scheme to her dad, she stretched out her feet in circles and stood. "I'd better join Jojo for a dance before he forgets he's married to me and not the music."

"Not likely." Crimson had seen the way the maire had looked at Ayla as she'd glided down the aisle. A small sigh left her lips. That was true love. There was no doubt in her mind now and her heart filled with warmth knowing that her friend had found love, even if it was with a dumpy satyr who used ten words when one would do.

"I believe it's traditional for the best man to dance with the bridesmaid." Lief appeared next to her and held out his hand. Crimson jumped. Stitches, he moved silently for someone so large.

Crimson smiled shyly and placed her hand in his, allowing Lief to pull her to her feet and lead her to the dance floor, where he pulled her close. The heat of his hands spread through her dress where he rested them on her waist.

He leaned in close. "You look beautiful."

She blushed, thankful for the dim lighting that hid her colouring cheeks. "You scrub up well yourself."

Lief swayed her in time with the music.

"Isn't this the wrong song for a slow dance?" Everyone else on the dancefloor moved in wilder motions, abandoning themselves to the beat in joyful celebration of the wedding thanks to the maire's magic. Crimson felt the compulsion to abandon reason and let go of her careful control. *And why not?* Ayla was happy. The dress was a success. The day had turned out well. Why not let go and enjoy herself? She leaned closer to Lief and rested her head on his chest.

"Does this mean we can be something more?" Lief asked, his breath hot against her ear.

Crimson looked up at him. She was done with putting her work first; it was time to have something for herself. It was time to explore where these feelings might take her and, yes, maybe even lose control a little. Crimson moved her arms up from his waist to the back of his head before pulling him down for a kiss, sure of what she wanted.

"Wait." Lief leaned his forehead against hers. "There's something I have to tell you first."

Chapter 38

~ A secret ~

"**S**ERIOUSLY?" CRIMSON BLINKED UP at Lief. What could be so important that he had to interrupt their second kiss?

Lief nodded, looked around, and swallowed. "Not here." He pulled her outside of the huge marquee and strode across the field, the green grass turned silver by the light of the gibbous moon that hung low in the night sky.

Crimson traipsed after him until they were almost at the hedge that marked the boundary with the neighbouring sheep field. Then she jerked her hand free, stopped and folded her arms. "I think we're far enough away that no one will hear us, unless you're worried about the ewes eavesdropping."

Lief glanced around and nodded. "I guess here will do." He

looked up at the sky. "I don't want there to be secrets between us, not if we're starting something. It's not fair." His voice, usually so sure, trembled.

"You're worrying me. Just come out and say it. It can't be worse than me thinking you were sleeping with your sister." Crimson tried to lighten the mood.

Lief raked his hands through his hair. "I don't know how to tell you this…so I think I'll have to show you." He took off his shirt.

Crimson took a step back. "What are you doing?" She glanced back at the tent. "What if someone comes out?"

Lief folded his shirt and placed it on the hedge before kicking off his shoes and putting them together in the grass.

"Lief, I think you should stop."

"You need to see this." He bent and pulled his trousers to the ground.

Crimson turned her back to him. Maybe it was prudish, maybe it was the city girl in her that was more up tight than the folk of Saffron Vale, but while she was theoretically fine with seeing someone naked, there was a time and a place for that. And at the back of the marquee where her best friend's wedding party was still in full swing did not count as the time or the place.

"Lief? Are you finished?"

No answer.

"OK, I'm going to turn around, but I want to make it very

clear that you need to cover yourself. Lief? Oh, for the Artisan's sake."

Crimson covered her eyes with her hands and turned round. The music from the party hummed a low beat in the background while the shrill squeaks of the fuzz bats swooping overhead hunting in the night sky sounded high above. Crimson's heartbeat pounded in her ears.

"Lief? Are you still there?"

A small chuff sounded from in front of her. A small, animal chuff. Crimson swallowed. Stitches. What game was Lief playing? What if a wild animal crept up on her? Was this standard courting in Saffron Vale; to leave someone alone in a field?

She parted her fingers a hair's breadth so she could peep through, expecting to see Lief grinning at her stupidity. Lief wasn't there. She removed her hands from her face and jumped back.

Sat, right where Lief had been undressing, right next to his shiny shoes, was a large wolf.

Crimson's eyes widened, and her heart raced.

The wolf cocked its head to one side.

Crimson mirrored it. "Are you the same wolf I saw in the forest? The one who walked me back home."

The wolf made a sound somewhere between a bark and a growl. Was that a yes?

"Where's Lief?"

The wolf made another noise in the back of its throat, almost like it was laughing at her.

Crimson stepped forward and narrowed her eyes, patching together memories like they were pattern pieces forming a cohesive garment when placed in the right way. "You're Lief?" There was still a question in her voice, a nervousness that this might be a practical joke and he would jump out from behind the hedge with a 'Got you!'.

It was the sort of joke that Namu, her childhood friend, would play on her. But Lief wasn't like him. He'd never been like him. Lief hadn't betrayed her. He'd only ever watched out for her, helped her, protected her.

"You walked me home."

The wolf – Lief – inclined his head.

She sank to the grass, not caring about the nighttime dew on her silk dress. "You protected me from the gang in the Capital."

The wolf padded over, towering over her small form. She hugged her arms around herself, not knowing how to take this.

Shifters lived in the queendom, of course they did, everyone knew that. But she'd never met one before. Never knowingly met one, she amended. They looked like everyone else most of the time and if someone was a little hairier than average, it wasn't considered polite to point that out. The Artisan knew she was grateful enough for the politeness of strangers when they didn't mention her rainbow flecked eyes or her teggish ancestry.

"I never said thank you." All this time and she hadn't known that Lief was her secret lupine protector. She met his animal gaze. "Thank you," she whispered.

He lay down next to her and Crimson threw her arms around his thick neck, burying her face in his soft silvery fur. "Thank you."

Now that she knew, it was obvious. The wolf had the same cinnamon brown eyes, and there was that brown tint to its silver fur, and if Lief had to be an animal, a wolf made perfect sense; a protector, someone who needed a pack. And he protected the whole of the vale from the dangers of the wild forest, as well as helping anyone who needed something doing with his strength and his skill.

Under her hands, his fur shortened, and his body morphed back into his human form, then his arms were round her and one hand stroked her hair.

"You're welcome, Red."

She lifted her head to meet his gaze. "Why didn't you just tell me?"

He shrugged, keeping her in his embrace. "I didn't know how."

"Does it hurt, when you…?"

"No. It's just part of who I am. It feels natural."

"And you don't need a full moon to…change?"

"Nope. But it does force the change. Twice a month, any time one of the twins is full." He tensed in her arms. "Does this…change anything for you? I won't blame you if it does. I know it's a lot to take in and if you're not comfortable with–"

Crimson pulled his face to hers and stopped his blabbering with a long kiss. "I know who you are, the form you take doesn't matter to me and I'm sorry you think that it would. I love you for who you are, not who you think you need to be."

"You love me?" he asked with a loopy grin.

"Maybe." Crimson smiled back at him. "We should get back to the party."

"Do we have to?"

Crimson swatted his muscular arm, and realised she was in the grass with a naked man. A very naked man. She pushed herself away from Lief and closed her eyes. "You have to get dressed!"

"Do I?"

"Yes! You have to give a speech! You're the best man! You can't be messing around outside while the speeches are happening." Crimson risked glancing at the sky, trying to judge the time from the height of the moon, but as she had no idea how to do that, she gave up.

"I thought the best man was supposed to mess around at the wedding," Lief said in a teasing tone. "Alright you can look. I'm decent."

Crimson glanced in his direction to see Lief buttoning up his shirt and slipping his shiny dress shoes back on.

He winced. "I won't be sorry to kick off these shoes for

good. How can anyone put up with them?"

"We have to go!"

Chapter 39

~ The speeches ~

THEY RACED INTO THE tent, skidded to a halt and Crimson attempted the sort of nonchalance one does when one wants to indicate that one has been here all along, thank you very much, and nothing untoward happened outside the tent. Particularly nothing involving naked men.

Just in time. Hardy stepped forward, motioned to the musicians to stop playing for a moment and the band's playing ended with a musical flourish.

"And now, the speeches. I believe it is traditional to start with the father of the bride." He gestured to Ayla's dad, who stepped forward and cleared his throat.

"Anyone who knows me knows I'm not big on speeches. So I just want to say that I can't believe this day has come, my baby Ayla all grown up and so beautiful." Ayla blushed and raised her glass to her dad. "It seems only yesterday she was a little elfling, playing with her pretend oven," his bright eyes turned misty and he wiped away a tear, "and now she's leaving me to join this excellent satyr. Or rather, I should say that I'm not losing Ayla, but am gaining a son. Come over here, son." He swept the maire into a tearful hug, bending down to embrace the smaller satyr. Ayla glided over and joined the family cuddle.

"Is that all?" whispered Hardy. Ayla's dad nodded, his face screwed up to stop the tears as Ayla patted him on the back and led him away from the stage. "Alright, that's it from the bride's father, now onto the groom. I present our maire; Jollivity Bowan."

Cheers rang out around the room and the maire detangled himself from Ayla's dad.

"Now, now, calm down everyone, as the priest said to the nuns." The drummer – a goblin who knew her business – added a 'boom, boom' to the end of the joke and drunken laughter rolled through the marquee. "As you all know, I can waffle on with the best of them."

"Hear, hear!"

"I know that was you, Hardy! So, before I get into it, I want to say how sumptuous my Ayla looks tonight. This gorgeous creature has deigned to marry me, and I pledge to her that I will do my utmost to make sure she never regrets that decision. To my bride!" The satyr raised his glass to the room, and everyone joined in the toast. "I haven't been this certain about something since the day I had the idea to revolutionise road travel with the curvy cart. I remember with utmost alacrity how I came upon the notion to add one cart behind another and double the load bearing capacity of the humble cart. It was a long winter's night, and I had laid aside the crossword–"

"Get on with it, you old goat!"

"Right, well yes, this is meant to be a party, not my ramblings about traffic convenience, even if it is the obvious next step in transportation. Anyhoozles, I want to thank the whole ruddy lot of you for making it today. It means the world to me and my wifikins that you could be here to witness our vows. And all that's left for me to say is that it's a free bar, so let's get sozzled!"

A raucous cheer reverberated around the tent and there was a concerted rush to the bar area where the cyclops from the Salt and Pickle Inn served drinks with varying degrees of alcohol content.

Hardy stepped forward again, straining to make his voice heard above the crowd around the bar. "Now, now everyone, if you please, we still have the best man's speech and, from everything I know about our humble maire, you won't want to miss this one."

With some shuffling of feet and much digging of ribs, the people in the marquee turned back to the stage where Lief shifted through a stack of papers he'd pulled from a pocket in his tailored suit. He coughed, began speaking in a hoarse voice, coughed again and took a drink that the lead singer offered him.

Crimson caught his eye. "Breathe." She demonstrated, taking a slow breath in and out. It was sweet, really, that this hulking specimen of a man – werewolf – should be so nervous about speaking in public. It made her want to rush over and lend him what little strength she had to steady his nerves. Instead, she settled for showing him how to take a deep breath.

It must have worked because Lief copied her and when next he spoke, his voice boomed around the tent.

"As a best man, I have three jobs; first to congratulate the happy couple." Lief raised his procured glass and the wedding guests followed suit. "To the bride and groom. And doesn't she look lovely everyone? Give us a twirl Ayla and show off that beautiful dress, not that you need it to look beautiful. Your dressmaker had an easy job of it with such a canvas to work on." He gave Crimson a wink, and she shook her head at him. That magnificent dress had cost her months of blood, sweat, and tears. Literally. But, by the Artisan, it looked amazing on Ayla.

Ayla spun slowly with a grin on her face. The maire looked up at her as if she were a goddess and he her humble priest, with so much devotion that Crimson had to look away; it was an intimate moment in front of everyone they knew.

"And really, you're too good for Jollivity. I don't know how he snared you, but if you need rescuing, blink twice."

A tear formed in the corner of her eye as Ayla strained to keep them open. The maire laughed and nudged the person next to him in the ribs.

"My second job as best man is to thoroughly embarrass the groom with tales of his days of ribald debauchery."

"Hear, hear!"

"Now, many of you know Jollivity Bowan only as the maire of Saffron Vale, but I have consulted with his friends – many of whom are here today–"

"Darn right we are!"

"Capital City boys forever!"

Lief waited until the cries from the maire's old chums had quieted down before he continued, "And you'll be pleased to know that they were eager to share their stories with me. Now, I can't share everything – some of the tales were far too saucy even for the not so innocent ears here today, like the time he stole the university mascot or that trip to Turtle Bay where I understand there were some misunderstandings with a group of kobolds...and I won't mention the lobster do sheep shenanigans..."

Loud guffaws cracked through the guests and the poor man standing next to the maire got another elbow to the ribs.

"So instead of tales about Jollivity's past, I thought I'd share the story of how he and Ayla met, as I was privileged enough to be there. We were all in Capital City – a delegation of us from Saffron Vale with varied purposes–"

"They never did take me up on my offer for the curvy cart manufacture," the maire said before Ayla shushed him.

"I happened to be escorting the lovely Crimson, who, incidentally, made Ayla's wedding gown–"

Someone wolf whistled, and the maire clapped.

"And we made our way to the market where it just so happened that her best friend had a stall selling the best bread in the Capital."

Ayla brushed off the compliment. Dilly downed her drink, and her brother placed a steadying hand on her shoulder.

"And, over the pastries and the crusty loaves, the eyes of this crusty old goat met those of this lovely elf and love filled the air in the form of overblown compliments which, I'm as shocked as you all are to say, Ayla seemed to enjoy.

"And there you have it, over the course of a smattering of days, a relationship was born and Ayla – for reasons unknown to the rest of us – followed him here to Saffron Vale and agreed to make an honest satyr out of him.

"I don't know much about love. I've chosen to live most of my life alone, on the outside of things, but I do know that Ayla and Jollivity are very lucky to have found each other, that they were brave enough to take the risk of falling in love and that they will have many happy years together. To the bride and groom and to love." He lifted his glass again and the words of his toast echoed around the marquee.

Lief took a sip of the sparkling wine and his smile turned wolfish. "Which leads me to my final role as best man…" Lief's gaze met Crimson's, "to kiss the bridesmaid."

Somehow a light shone on Crimson, exposing her to the wedding guests. Darn those spotlight mirrors.

Crimson's blush spread from the tip of her toes in her stockinged feet to the very top of her head where her hair had tumbled from its elaborate up do. She made no move as Lief stalked over, cradled her face between his hands, and brushed his thumb over her bottom lip.

Crimson let out a small gasp. He leaned forward and planted a chaste kiss on her lips. The wedding guests went wild.

Maire Bowan skipped back to the front of the stage. "And now, ladies and gentlemen, beasts and beauties, let's really get this party started. I give you the one, the only – you know who it is – Sibby!"

Chapter 40

~ *The day after* ~

CRIMSON JOLTED UPRIGHT. STITCHES. There was too much to do. The wedding…was yesterday. With a groan she collapsed back onto her bed. It was over. Her friend was happy and married. Even now, they were probably setting off on their honeymoon.

Ayla had insisted that elves needed a year long honeymoon as they lived for so long and the maire had been only too happy to agree. They planned to tour the queendom and visit some of the maire's friends along the way.

Crimson stretched out and tickled Smudge under his ear when he climbed onto the bed. Some things never changed. She got up to let Smudge out for his morning constitutional.

A banging sounded through her head, shaking her skull. She groaned again. She hadn't had that much to drink, and she'd stayed away from the deceptive scrumpy. It took her a moment to realise that the banging came from the door.

Who in the queendom wanted dressmaking services at this time of day? She opened the door ready to turn whoever it was away. It was the day after the wedding and she deserved a break, didn't she?

"Morning." Lief leaned against the door, bright eyed and smiling in the morning sunshine. "Did you sleep well?"

Crimson stifled a yawn. "What are you doing here?" She was too tired to be polite.

"It's after the wedding…"

She paused by the counter. He didn't mean to jump right into a relationship now, did he? Not when all she wanted to do was curl up and go back to sleep.

"So, I thought you should relax."

The tension that had gathered in Crimson's shoulders eased, and she sighed. "That is exactly what I want to do today."

"Perfect. Then come with me."

Crimson turned and looked into his puppy dog eyes and found herself telling him that she just needed to get dressed. With another yawn, she returned downstairs to find Smudge sitting at Lief's feet.

"Grab your design book."

"My design book? No, I just want to relax." She rubbed her eyes.

"Just in case."

"Fine." Crimson grabbed her book from where it lay on the counter and stomped out of the door. "Happy now?"

"Drink this."

Crimson sniffed the flask with suspicion. The sharp notes of peppermint and sugar might hide something like that awful hangover cure which she definitely did not need.

"It's tea. A pick me up from Dilly."

"That doesn't reassure me." Crimson grumbled but she took a sip and sighed at the warming sensation that filled her body. Dilly might be a pain about knowing which teas were best for people, but in this instance, she was right. Crimson felt her stiff muscles relax and her body shed the tiredness as she drank. "Thank you," she said, her mood lightening after the tea. "What now?" The sooner this was over with, the sooner she could go back to bed. Her cheeks heated as she thought about her bed while next to this man.

"Now we walk."

Crimson's stomach rumbled. "I hope that basket contains some food." That would distract her from her wayward thoughts.

Lief laughed and handed her a breakfast croissant before heading towards the forest. Crimson ate most of it, savouring the flaky pastry before she handed the end to Smudge, who snapped it up and raced ahead to beg for more food from Lief.

As they left the town and followed the meandering path

towards the river, Crimson relaxed further. The temperature was perfect, not too hot, not too cold. She took a deep breath. The air was fresh, she couldn't even smell the ever-present tang of gone off fish.

She crinkled her nose. That wasn't true. It was still there, along with the salty undercurrent that hung over the vale, but she didn't notice it anymore. Maybe she was a local now.

A warm fuzziness blanketed her as Crimson thought she might actually belong somewhere. It felt…comfortable, like a warm fleece on a cold day or knitted stockings that fit perfectly. Maybe that could be the theme of her next collection; comfort.

She paused and opened her design book to jot that down. Yes, and she could find the softest, fluffiest materials and make them look chic. Perhaps cardigans and oversized slouchy jumpers that draped down to people's knees.

And the colour palette…Crimson looked up and her gaze caught on the soft meadow flowers that still lined the path in the autumn season. Pastels? That could work.

A leaf danced across the path, taken by the wind as it fell from the tree. Crimson bent to pick up one of its fallen comrades. Or autumn hues of umbers, chestnut browns, pumpkin oranges, yellows, burnt reds? Colours that reminded her of warm fires on cold days and staying indoors. A smile curved her lips. Yes, autumn would be her inspiration for the colours. She would have to speak to Ig about how rich he could get the dyes.

She picked another leaf, this one a soft speckled yellow, and tucked it into her book.

And so the morning passed with Crimson building her collection of autumn leaves. Lief tried to help, but after he picked up a leaf covered in what she hoped was mud and not fox poo, Crimson asked him to stop.

They reached the small promontory by the river and Lief spread the faded tartan blanket that covered his wicker basket out on the grass.

Crimson sat, and sketched out the tartan pattern in her book, not sure if she would use it, but the interwoven lines of thread were fascinating.

"And now, I present lunch." Lief unpacked the basket and pulled out venison pie, breaded eggs and a rich chocolate cake topped with scarlet strawberries.

"All my favourites." Crimson sighed with happiness.

"I know." Lief dished up the food and they sat watching the river as they ate.

Crimson knew this was the start of something, but she wasn't sure exactly what. She knew Lief's secret now, not that there was any shame in being a shifter, and she'd promised they'd talk after the wedding, but what to say? And how to say it?

She couldn't blurt out that she was interested in him and wanted to have a relationship. If he still wanted to. Did he still want her? They had kissed, but he might have been under the influence of alcohol and the romance of the wedding. Maybe she'd misread things, and he'd brought her here to tell her he'd changed his mind.

"Everything alright?" Lief quirked one of those dark eyebrows at her, and Crimson's stomach fluttered.

She nodded and took a large bite of the pie, so she didn't have to reply. Better to watch the river and wait for a better time instead of overthinking things. The foam sprite had said she needed to loosen her laces to be happy…

Crimson undid her boots and tucked them to the side of the blanket before tucking her stockinged feet underneath her. There, that was more comfortable at least.

After the savouries, Crimson sat on her hands to stop her reaching for the chocolate cake that called her name from across the rug. She managed to resist its lure for all of thirty seconds.

"Shall we have the cake now?" she asked.

Lief took out a knife, ready to cut it when he pointed to the river. "Did you see the rainbow trout?"

Crimson turned her head in the direction of the splash, but the fish had already gone. "Great, you saw a fish. Now how about that cake?"

"Anticipation is part of the pleasure," Lief said, holding the knife over the cake.

Crimson blushed and bit her lip as he handed her a generous slice, allowing his fingers to brush hers and sending a rising heat spreading across her skin. She turned her attention back to the food and the river, too unsure of herself to know where this was heading.

As she licked the last of the rich, chocolate icing from her fingers, Lief made a choking sound.

"Is everything alright?" she asked.

"How's your day of relaxation going?" He avoided the question.

"Perfect." Crimson leaned back and closed her eyes, tipping her head back in the autumn sunshine. She was full of her favourite foods, and her mind brimmed with inspiration for her new collection.

"Not quite. I brought you something else to complete your relaxation." Lief dug around in the basket and pulled out a romance book. "Happy ever after guaranteed. I checked with the shopkeeper."

Crimson bit her lip to stop her giggle as she imagined the hulking Lief asking about romance books; they didn't seem like his usual read. "You did that? For me?"

He nodded. "Is it what you wanted? I tried to get everything right, but I was worried I'd forgotten something when you told me about your perfect day." Lief's brow crinkled as he rummaged through the basket. "I got this one too, in case you didn't like that book, or you'd already read it."

"How many books did you buy?"

"Five," he mumbled, not meeting her gaze.

Crimson did laugh this time and reached over to look in the basket. Some of the covers made her blush. Suddenly, she was aware of her closeness to him and time seemed to stand still. This was her moment. She cupped his cheek and drew him down so she could press his lips to hers.

He pulled away and searched her face. "Are you sure?"

She nodded. She was sure of this. More sure than she had been about anything.

Lief leaned in and kissed her, his fingers running through her hair. "You belong here, with me."

Crimson's heart swelled with happiness, contentment, love. She belonged. And then she didn't think of much else for quite some time.

~

If you want to read about the maire's lobster do from Lief's point of view, then you can find the full story here: https://books.gemmaclatworthy.com/commission-impossible

Found a typo? Drop G Clatworthy an email at:
gemma@gemmaclatworthy.com

Thank you

A special thank you to my amazing patrons: Emma Ward, ZomBev and Sueann Snow who always support me.

If you want to support Gemma, you can find her on www.patreon.com/G_Clatworthy for exclusive first reads of new stories.

You can also join her newsletter at www.gemmaclatworthy.com for a free prequel to the Saffron Vale series and follow Gemma on www.instagram.com/gemmaclatworthy, www.facebook.com/gemmaclatworthy or join the Facebook reader's group Gemma's book wyrms.

Other Books by G Clatworthy

Books in the Saffron Vale series:

A Colour to Dye For

Going for Guild

Commission Impossible

Books in the Rise of the Dragons series:

Awakening

Solstice of Dragons

Equinox Betrayal

Darkest Deception

Attack on Avalon

Fated Bloodlines

Books in the Omensford series (set in the Rise of the Dragons universe):

Bedsocks and Broomsticks

Cream Teas and Crystal Balls

Donkeys and Demons

Pumpkins and Popstars

Exes and Enchantments

Fae and Familiars

Gnomes and Necromancy

Books in the Vampire Graduate Scheme series (set in the Rise of the Dragons universe):

Placement One: Fae Audits

Placement Two: The Archives

Placement Three: Executive Assistant

Children's Books

The Child Who series:

   The Girl Who Lost Her Listening Ears

   The Boy Who Lost His Listening Ears

   The Girl Who Dreamed of Sleep

   The Boy Who Dreamed of Sleep

Nanny Pastry series:

Nanny Pastry and the Nimble Ninjabread Man

Other books:

Coronavirus in the words of children

About the Author

Gemma started writing during the 2020 lockdown and loves fantasy fiction and dragons in particular. She lives in Wiltshire with her family and two cats and also enjoys crafts of all kinds. You can read all her writing first on www.patreon.com/G_Clatworthy.

Or join the conversation at Gemma's book wyrms readers' group on Facebook.

She also writes children's books. You can find out more on her website www.gemmaclatworthy.com or follow her on Instagram (www.instagram.com/gemmaclatworthy) or Facebook (www.facebook.com/gemmaclatworthy).

www.gemmaclatworthy.com